ID0984607

MURDER IN TINSELTOWN

MURDER IN TINSELTOWN

EARL HAMNER & DON SIPES

HAWK PUBLISHING

Published in the United States by HAWK Publishing Group.

HAWK and colophon are trademarks belonging to the
HAWK Publishing Group.

Printed in the United States of America.

Library of Congress Cataloging in Publication Data
Hamner, John, and Sipes, Don
Murder in Tinseltown/Earl Hamner and Don Sipes–
HAWK Publishing ed.
p. cm.
ISBN 1-930709-15-3
1.Fiction–California
2. Fiction–Hollywood
I. Title
[PS3563.I42145R4 2000]
813'.54   80-52413
CIP

HAWK Publishing web address: www.hawkpub.com

H987654321

CURTIS HUGHES' JOURNAL

I think I'd go crazy without this journal. When I used to tell people how I felt about Ariel they would laugh and make fun of me so I learned to keep my innermost feelings to myself. She hasn't worked lately, not since she had that running role on Guiding Light. *Even then she wasn't happy—and no wonder—the writers never gave her enough to do. I have written to the producers of* Kings Harbor *ever since I read in the trades that she was up for the role of Tiffany. Of course, like everybody else, they never acknowledge my letters, but she is right for the role and I will do anything to see that she gets it. She is so much better than any of the other actresses in the running for the role. Especially Lyla Taylor. Trash! Trash! Trash!*

CHAPTER ONE

I t was the usual busy night at the Ivy. Curbside valet attendants were busy wheeling off one expensive car after another as they drew up to the entrance on Robertson Boulevard. Customers in the patio dining area divided their attention between the Louisiana crab cakes and the steady stream of personalities arriving to see and be seen.

In the interior, tastefully decorated to resemble a French farm house, nobody was eating. They were too busy looking to see who was at the next table. It was rumored that Madonna and her party had reservations for later in the evening, and diners lingered over their key lime pie, hoping for a prime celebrity sighting.

Emory Goode made his usual commanding entrance, with a spectacular young woman clinging to his arm. Every eye in the restaurant turned to watch him make his way to his table. Even those who had no idea that he was one of the most important directors in the business looked at him and were impressed.

His expansive six-foot-two frame was clad as usual in a white linen suit, adorned only by a black string tie at the throat of his plain white shirt. Emory affected a costume he had copied from an old family photograph dominated by his great-grandfather, who had been a well-to-do merchant in Nashville, Tennessee. Emory's aristocratic ancestors had fought with distinction in the

American Revolution and after the war had emigrated to Nashville, where they prospered. The family still looked at Emory with wonder and slight disapproval that he had chosen the entertainment industry over the family business.

Emory enjoyed the effect his appearance created. In New York it had attracted even more attention than here in California, where bizarre costuming was taken for granted. He carried a planter's hat which he'd removed as he entered the restaurant.

Such an arrogant display of plumage demanded a sizable talent to justify it. Emory Goode had that talent. Until recently he had been disdainful of television, preferring to work instead on the New York or London stage. But a separation had caused many changes in his life, not the least of which was a need for quick, hard cash. His wife had moved back to her native California bringing their teenaged daughter Robin with her. Robin had been a heartache for the last two years and that, too, had been a factor in Emory's move to the West Coast.

Emory had been offered the direction of a dramatic television pilot for IBC, one of the top television networks. It was to be filmed by the gigantic independent production company, Porter Productions. To its list of several successful series the head of production, Max Porter, hoped to add *King's Harbor*. In the genre of *Dallas* and *Falcon Crest*, *King's Harbor* was set in the affluent Orange County city of Newport Beach. It featured the usual themes of the struggle for wealth and sexual gratification.

Emory took in the room with a slow, deliberate, appraising glance. He was always amused at the pretensions of Los Angelenos. Few appreciated the good meat loaf and fried chicken, specialties of the chef; for most, the location of their table or the reputation of the restaurant was more important.

Emory's companion wore a black sheath split nearly to her hip, and her sensual stride exhibited a generous amount of thigh. She carried herself as if she had no idea of the attention she was attracting. She gave her entire attention to Emory, smiling and nodding at his every remark as if everything he said was fresh, direct, original and brilliant.

Which it often was.

"I'll have my usual, Tim," he said to the handsome young waiter who had materialized promptly as though he'd been waiting for the director to take his seat. Like most waiters in Hollywood, Tim was an out-of-work actor and paid special attention to customers who were involved in the business.

"And the lady?" Tim asked, trying not to leer at the exposed expanse of flesh.

"I'll have the same," she said.

Tim said with an engaging smile, "Only one sazarac to a customer. I'm supposed to tell you that."

She replied, "Whatever," and turned her adoring gaze back to Emory.

Emory looked at her with candid appraisal. Lyla Taylor, he knew, had come from poverty in the backwoods of Mississippi and had fled to New York one step ahead of an abusive husband whom she'd married at sixteen. In New York she found another man who had sponsored her education and welfare in exchange for her favors. Neither were disappointed in the bargain. She had disengaged from her benefactor and become a working, if not totally successful, New York actress by the time Emory first met her and cast her in a small role in a play he was directing.

Lyla had asked for this dinner. Emory surmised what she had in mind. She had a certain cheapness which would make her appropriate for the role he would be casting in *King's Harbor*, and he resolved to let her play out her hand to see how she would handle it.

"I admire your way of going after what you want," he said.

"Then you know what I want?" she asked. "The role of Tiffany is ready-made for me. I've been waiting for this role most of my life."

"I'll admit you have just the right touch of . . ." When he hesitated, she supplied the proper word, "Sluttishness."

"Well, yes, but she's more than that."

"So am I," she rejoined. "What do I have to do to get the role?"

Briefly their knees touched under the table. By accident or by design he couldn't tell, but he slowly moved his leg closer to his chair. She seemed not to notice.

"You have to audition like any other actress."

"I know Ariel Smart has already tried out. How did she do?"

"Professional courtesy doesn't allow me to share that."

"She has much too virginal a look for the role," Lyla said.

"Casting against type can be interesting though," Emory said. "Remember in New York when I cast you as Laura in *The Glass Menagerie*?"

"Definitely against type, but I was younger." She leaned in close enough to catch the scent of an expensive male cologne.

"What is that?" she asked.

"What's what?"

"That cologne. It's wonderful."

"It's not a cologne. It's a special soap that's made for me in a small town in Provence."

"I like it," she said. "It's very masculine."

"They put a lot of citrus and mint in it."

Just then drinks arrived. They clinked glasses, sipped, and relaxed for a moment.

"Strong," she said. "What's in it?"

"Mostly bourbon," he said. "With just a touch of pernod. Be careful. It can lead into dangerous waters."

"I'm a good swimmer." She raised her glass again. People at nearby tables smiled at the handsome couple, wondering what they were celebrating.

"Here's to our working together," she said.

"First, you audition," he said firmly.

They looked up when a male voice said, "Excuse me, Emory, I just wanted to say hello."

"Hello," Emory said with a blank look. A small, seedy-looking man was holding out his hand for Emory to shake. He did not remember the man or his name, and he ignored the proffered handshake.

"Marty Miller."

"Oh, of course," said Emory, "the producer."

"Agent," he said with a slight smile.

Miller was a small-time agent. His suit looked as if it had been cut down from a larger man's size. He had left the William Morris Agency ten years ago, taking with him a modest group of clients who had all gradually drifted away. It was well known in the industry that Marty had fallen on hard times. He presented himself, as always, on the verge of making an enormous deal which somehow never came to fruition.

"I hear you're doing the *King's Harbor* pilot," Marty said.

"And what do the gossips say to that?" Emory asked, knowing the gossips were saying he had abandoned the New York theater because he needed the money. But then money was what brought everybody to the film capital.

"They say the show is lucky to have you," Marty simpered with a kiss-ass smile. "I'd go along with that," Emory responded. He knew what Marty was doing. It was behavior expected of agents. "By the way, I'd like you to meet Miss Lyla Taylor."

"We've met," Marty said with a nod of recognition to Lyla. She nodded back coldly, but made no further acknowledgment.

"How do you two know each other?" Emory asked.

"I used to represent Lyla," he said.

"Yes, for about fifteen minutes."

The tips of Marty's ears turned red for a moment, but he managed a weak smile and turned back to the director.

"One of my clients is in line for the role of Tiffany," Marty said.

"Oh, which one?" Emory asked.

"Ariel Smart," he answered.

Lyla turned toward Emory and rolled her eyes heavenward.

"Good actress," said Emory. His companion kicked him under the table.

"I hear the role's been taken," Lyla said.

"No," said Emory. "The role's not been cast yet."

"It probably will be before the night's over."

"All I ask is you give my client a chance. She's perfect for the role, and it'd be a good idea to grab her while she's available because "ER" wants her for a multiple guest role."

Yeah, right, Emory thought. "We shall see," he said, and went back to his sazarac with a gesture that indicated the conversation was over.

"Have a good day," Marty said as he moved on to another table and another producer he was wooing.

"Likewise," Emory said.

"Pathetic," Lyla commented after Marty had left.

Emory said, "He's seen better days."

"Yeah, he represented Judas at the Last Supper."

"Have a little pity," Emory said. "You have to feel sorry for people like that. The film industry turns its back on them, and there's no way they can make a living."

"He didn't get me a single interview," Lyla said indignantly, "let alone a job."

"Shame he can't find some other way to make a living."

"He won't give up agenting. I hear he operates out of a little cubbyhole in Culver City ten miles from any major studio. And the only clients he can pick up are girls who just got into town and are still wet behind the ears. All he's got besides the kids just off the bus are a few old timers from the waxworks who are just getting over their bypass operations."

Emory looked at the girl wonderingly. In New York, actors seemed to feel a fellowship with each other. He had not found that out here. He attributed it to the competitive nature of the business and the huge rewards that an actor could gain by besting a colleague for the role.

"Now, let's understand each other," Emory said. "Why do you think you're ready to play Tiffany?"

"I'm right for the part. I got hold of the script, and I've got it memorized. I'd love to show you what I can do!"

"Aside from that," Emory said, wondering if he should tell her that if she were less aggressive she might advance her career more readily.

"I am Tiffany," she said.

"Tiffany is not a very nice girl."

"Well, I'm no angel," she said.

Emory said, "I didn't take you for one," and beckoned to the waiter. Tim arrived almost immediately with menus.

"May I tell you about the specials this evening?" he asked. At Emory's nod he launched into his recitation.

"I have Chilean sea bass with a mustard lime glaze. I serve that with fresh steamed spinach and couscous. Our Orange Roughy this evening is crusted with shredded cornflakes and pepper. Really good and arrived from New Zealand just this morning by air."

"I was under the impression it swam over," Emory said. Tim pretended he didn't mind the interruption.

"And of course we always have the fried chicken, meat loaf, crab cakes and red snapper prepared Creole style."

"The snapper fly in too?" asked Emory.

"No, it swam," Tim answered with a grin.

"I'll just have a small, green salad," said Lyla. "I'm watching my figure."

"So's everybody else in the restaurant," Emory said.

"Really," she answered. "I hadn't noticed."

"We also have one order of gingered catfish left," Tim said.

"I'll have it," Emory said, "But I want it prepared with olive oil instead of butter."

As the waiter left the table with their order, Lyla observed, "Nice buns."

"Are you a connoisseur of such anatomical assets?" he smiled.

"I appreciate them," she said. "I admire the best, and his definitely are right up there. He'll go far in the business. Of course, he's an actor."

"Isn't every waiter in Los Angeles? Now as you were saying," Emory observed, "you think you're right for the role of Tiffany."

"I'd like to audition just for you," Lyla said.

"Well, I've given Ariel Smart a reading, I suppose I owe you the same consideration."

"Where did she read?"

"On the set."

"I'd like that, too."

"Then we'll arrange a reading for tomorrow. No, I've got to go on a location hunt tomorrow. It'll have to be later in the week."

"I don't want to wait. What's wrong with tonight?"

Emory felt a moment of resistance. He was keeping his daughter's white Labrador retriever and the dog was waiting for its evening walk.

"I suppose we could, but we'll have to make it quick," he said against his better judgment. Lyla could be right for the role, but she would be a hard sell unless the casting director agreed with him, and she would not be present if they read tonight. Nevertheless, he decided to go along with Lyla's wish.

"I could get the studio guards to unlock the sound stage. The set's still up. We'll run out there right after we finish dinner."

When Tim brought the check Lyla reached for it, but Emory intercepted it.

"I'm taking you to dinner," she said.

"Next time," he promised.

"When are you going to let me try out for a part, Mr.

Goode?" Tim asked as he collected the check.

"When I find one for a good-looking young waiter."

"I'd rather play the good-looking lifeguard," said Tim.

"I'll keep you in mind, Tim." said Emory. "Miss Taylor tells me you're eminently qualified."

At the curb, waiting for their cars to be brought around, Lyla noticed a clean-cut, All-American boy, one of the parking attendants, gazing at her with a malevolent stare. When he walked toward her to take her claim check she noticed that he had a slight limp, but what shone most was his look of pure hatred.

"What are you looking at, you prick?"

He blushed and turned away. As he walked away it appeared to Emory that the boy was trying not to limp.

Emory heard Lyla's remark and it confirmed his conviction that she had no real compassion and was probably just right for the role of Tiffany. She was just trashy enough to fit the role.

On the way to the studio, Emory called the security office and requested that they leave the door open and some lights on on Stage 23. He informed the guard that he and Lyla Taylor would be arriving in separate cars.

When he arrived at the entrance to the studio the guard recognized Emory and waved him on through.

"The lady said she'd be waiting for you at the stage," the guard called.

"Thanks, Frank," Emory replied. Emory had learned the importance of cultivating the guard at the gate. They operated like small-time nobles admitting peasants to the royal court. Sometimes they refused admittance, and there was a legend that one of them had even shot a person who attempted to enter without authorization.

The studio lot, lit only by an occasional overhead street light, was deserted and looked like a scene in a movie just before the monster arrives and wreaks havoc. Although Emory knew the lot by day, it often gave him a chilled feeling at this hour of the night.

The stage was the size of an airplane hangar. Lyla was waiting just inside the door. Their footsteps echoed through the ghostly, silent building until they came at last to an island of light which bathed the living room set of *King's Harbor*. The set had been designed by a top Hollywood designer and far exceeded in expense and style the sets for *Dynasty* and *Dallas*. Through the wide bay window was a painted backdrop of the Pacific. A 50-foot yacht rested on the painted ocean and royal palms lined a causeway down to the private pier. On camera it would appear as real and lavish as any dock off Palm Beach or Newport.

"Is there anything about *King's Harbor* you'd like me to know before I read for the part?" Lyla asked.

"It's set in a ritzy enclave on the Orange County Coast like Newport. The King Family once owned most of Orange County, and now there's a struggle by the descendants of the family for control of the empire. The two contenders are sisters. One, Amanda King, lives in a compound on Lido Island. The other lives on the family hacienda in the Inland Empire. The two sisters are locked in continual warfare to best each other and gain control of a fortune that would match an Arabian oil dynasty."

"I know that," she said. "I read the script."

"The present plot line has Amanda King trying to find the daughter she gave birth to 22 years ago. That's the Tiffany part you're trying out for. Except we're not sure it's Tiffany."

"Where has my character been all that time?"

"After she was born her mother wanted to keep the child and make her the heiress to the King fortune, but her sister had the child abducted and spirited away to New Orleans. The girl is now in her early twenties and has reason to believe she may be the missing King daughter."

"Should I do a Southern accent in the audition?"

"No, just be natural. Try to give the character a feeling of mystery."

"When did Ariel Smart do her audition?"

"Last week." Emory looked at his watch. This was taking longer than he had planned.

"She was probably good. I know her work."

"Never worry about the competition. Just do the best you can."

"Do you want to direct me in the scene?" Lyla asked.

"No, I'd like to see what you can do with it on your own. Show me your vision of the character."

Emory began setting the stage for the scene. This was a part of the job he enjoyed, the feeling of control, of creativity, of interpreting human behavior.

"Pretend I'm the camera. I'll be here. I'm not going to interrupt you. If you forget a line, ad lib something. In the scene, you're meeting the woman you think is your mother for the first time. Let's see what you can do."

Lyla walked to the center of the pool of light. Something new, something from inside where her talent resided came forward, and she was transformed into an imaginary person who had been created by a writer, but was nonetheless real at that moment.

"Very touching," called Emory when she reached the end of the audition scene. It occurred to him again that the girl actually did have the right quality for the role.

"Do I stand a chance?" she asked.

"Better than a chance. You caught the character perfectly. Now we'd better go. It's getting late."

"Oh, look" she exclaimed. "There's the bedroom set."

"What about it?" asked Emory, one step ahead of her, half knowing why her sudden interest in the bedroom set.

"Don't try to seduce me, my dear," he said. "I don't do business that way."

"I'd do anything to get this job."

"I'm well aware," he said. "Now we'll be going. Audition's over."

"Have I got the job?" she persisted.

"As far as I'm concerned you've got the job, but you'll still have to audition for the network. I'm taking you and Ariel over to the network tomorrow. You'll both read for Gerald Walker and the casting director. I will recommend you. I'm not too crazy about you as a person, but you're a natural for the role. You made it resonate."

"Then it's yes."

"You still have to try out at the network, but my advice has a lot of weight."

"You're going to think I'm a kook, but I really need this job. If you don't mind, I want to memorize every inch of the set so when I try out for the network tomorrow it's like home. You don't have to wait for me."

"Are you sure you're comfortable here alone? These old sound stages are haunted, you know. Barbara Stanwyck comes here every night. So does Claude Rains. He swings in from a rope, still wearing his "Phantom of the Opera" make-up. Olivia de Havilland peers over that balcony up there singing 'Hush, Hush, Sweet Charlotte.' All those ghosts."

"They don't frighten me. Thanks for feeding me and thanks for being on my side."

"Good night," he said.

Coming out of the stage door Emory saw that the light was burning in the office of Justin Hargreaves, the writer and creator of *King's Harbor*. He thought of a few lines of dialogue he wanted added to the script.

"Anybody here?" he called.

The pounding of conputer keys grew stronger as he went

toward a modest, windowless office at the very end of the hall.

Sitting at the desk was a dark-haired slim man in his early thirties. Even seated it was obvious that he was quite tall. His face was lean and his hazel eyes appeared intelligent, but tired and preoccupied at the moment. He was so wrapped up in his writing that he had not heard Emory enter.

Emory had met the writer and decided he would have to handle him with care. He was stubborn, a sullen, sensitive young man, convinced that he was underpaid, underappreciated, over-worked, insulted and scorned by actors and fellow workers alike. He also felt that the concept for every successful series on the air had been stolen from him.

"Burning the midnight oil, I see," said Emory.

Justin's smudged glasses gave him a studious look. His desk was unexpectedly neat and orderly for the desk of a writer turning out vast numbers of words in a day. He was startled by the sudden appearance of Emory.

"Know where I can hire a good writer?" he asked.

"I hope you're not quitting."

"No, I'm tired. I'm doing the work of a whole writing team."

Emory was aware that most writers resented directors, and it was true that most directors fought for and won important pos-sessory credits. Possessory credits such as "A film by so-and-so" had come into vogue from the European film industry, where directors had called themselves "auteurs." The credit implied that theirs was the overriding creative contribution on which the picture was based. Writers also aspired to those credits, but few had been able to obtain them. From its inception, the film indus-try had relegated writers to the lowest rank, and writers still suf-fered from this onus.

"That's true," Emory agreed, "But nobody knows these char-acters the way you do. It's your baby, and nobody can write this stuff but you."

"What are you doing roaming around this hour of the night?"

"I auditioned an actress down on the set. I've pretty much decided on casting Tiffany. I'll let the boss know in the morning before we go to the network."

"You've picked Ariel Smart, of course."

"That would be on-the-nose casting. She's good, but Lyla Taylor has a certain quirky quality I'm looking for. She's down on the set right now soaking up atmosphere."

"I want Ariel," Justin said. His assertion came with such force that he seemed to surprise even himself.

Emory was surprised at the heated statement. Writers were not normally involved in casting the roles even though they had created them.

"Oh, we'll find something else for Ariel."

"But I'm writing the role of Tiffany for Ariel. She's been my model for the role ever since I created the part. I want people to like Tiffany. She has an air of innocence, and that's what Ariel Smart delivers."

"That's not the way I see Tiffany," Emory replied. "Underneath it all she's a tramp, and that's how I want the audience to see her."

"You tell me the show is my baby, and at the same time you're trying to kill it." Justin got up from his desk and began stalking around the room. "Lyla Taylor is trash! I'll stop you from casting her any way I can."

"I'm directing this picture, and you'll have to trust my judgment. Is something going on between you and Ariel?"

Emory was sorry he had asked the question. He could see the anger and resentment rising all over again.

"I wish there were," Justin said. His voice began to tremble.

"Then why don't you just write in a role for Ariel?" suggested Emory.

"If we miscast Tiffany we're going to ruin the pilot, and we could lose the show altogether. She's the key," he argued.

"Trust me," Emory said. He used the cliché on purpose hoping to amuse Justin and lighten his wrath.

It didn't work. Emory was astonished at the rage that rose and burst forth from the writer. His whole body trembled. His eyes grew red with anger and frustration.

"I won't let you do this to my show!" he screamed. "You'll be sorry for this, Emory!"

"My boy, calm yourself," warned Emory. He backed away, but Justin followed him all the way to the exit, screaming obscenities.

CHAPTER TWO

The young man drove past the gate to the studio several times before he decided on a course of action. Each time he passed the gate and saw the guard he knew he had to find another way to get on the lot.

He had come prepared. He parked his car on a side street away from the street light and made his way to the wall which went around the entire studio.

He had been on the lot before and knew from the contours of the building that it was the storage shed where old flats used in the construction of sets were stored. They were as dry as tinder.

He checked his pocket once again to make sure the knife was still there. He hoped he would have the strength to carry out what he felt he had to do. He'd never realized love could be such a burden.

The very first match did the trick. He watched as the small flame began to lick its way up the dry, canvas-covered flat which had once been used in a movie about Morocco.

He waited for the chaos that was sure to ensue.

On the hillside overlooking the studio Emory Goode was walking his daughter's white Lab, Oscar. Emory had taken him in when his daughter and her mother moved into an apartment that didn't allow pets. He'd become fond of the dog and looked forward to their rambles each night and morning.

Oscar lunged at something along the dark path and Emory restrained the dog by its leash. Up ahead, a coyote scampered down the roadway.

From where he stood Emory could see the studio he'd just left and as he looked his attention was attracted to a flaring light. He suddenly realized the studio was on fire. For a moment he considered going back to see if his set was endangered, but as he watched more closely he saw that the flames came from a far corner of the studio where sets were stored, nowhere near the *King's Harbor* sound stage.

Nevertheless he rushed into the apartment and called the security office.

"Wilbur, it's Emory Goode," he said. "Are you aware that there's a fire on the lot?"

"Good God, no," said the head of Security.

"Looks like it's down around the storage area, and it's growing bigger by the minute."

"Thanks," said the guard and hurriedly put in an emergency call to the fire department, speaking as though he had just discovered the fire himself. He could lose his job if it came out that the fire had been pointed out by someone off the lot.

Within moments fire trucks were creating confusion and chaos on the lot. One moment it had seemed almost deserted; in the next, night crews and workers preparing for tomorrow's filming came swarming out of offices, kitchens, paint shops and guards kiosks. For a while, studio security broke down as guards rushed to help put out the fire. Anybody could have walked right onto the lot.

For a few minutes after Emory left, Lyla simply wandered around the set, marveling at the detail of its design. Through the bay window the sun almost sparkled on the painted ocean and the ship seemed to rock gently at its moorings.

She rehearsed her scene several times. She heard the sounds of sirens in the distance, but she did not let them interrupt her concentration. When she felt satisfied with the scene and decided it was time to go, she heard a sound that came from inside the sound stage. It sounded like a footstep. She walked to the edge of the lighted area and peered into the darkness. A little chill of apprehension went up her spine.

She assured herself that it was only her imagination at work. When the sound came again, closer this time, she called "Who's there?" Her voice quavered just a little. At the far end of the sound stage she plainly saw the red exit light. She would have to traverse an immense dark area, but she had to get to that light.

As she stepped into the darkness, the footsteps sounded again, behind her now, and she broke into a run. Reaching the exit door, she grasped the handle and pulled desperately but the door would not move. She tried to shake it open.

Looking back to the set she realized she had seen a telephone there. Once again she raced through the darkened sound stage, her heart pounding, her throat dry with fear. She reached the phone, picked it up. The line was dead.

Suddenly she felt someone immediately behind her. Hysterically she ran to the bay window which looked out on the artificial harbor. She clutched at the window as if it were real, and then she turned. She found herself face to face with Bette Davis. The last thing she saw was Bette's hand holding the knife as it descended in the first of a series of violent slashes.

CHAPTER THREE

Morning dawned in a cloud of pink and grey clouds over the San Gabriel mountains. Gradually the shadows shortened as the sun rose higher over the parched chaparral. Another hot day was beginning in Los Angeles.

Wilbur Cross wasn't supposed to sleep while on duty. His father, a veteran of World War Two, had claimed that in his day if you fell asleep on guard duty you could get yourself shot. The excitement of the fire and the stress of the aftermath had exhausted Wilbur, and toward dawn he dozed off in spite of himself.

He woke with a start and looked at the digital clock on his desk. He brought his feet down from where they had been propped and rose to his feet, stifled a last yawn, and headed out in the first light of the new day. He yawned and rubbed the stubble on his cheeks. A shave and a shower would feel wonderful along about now. He usually kept up his appearance better than this, but the last twelve hours had left no time for keeping up appearances. The smell of smoke and wet, smoldering timber still hung over the studio as he emerged into the morning air.

He was late making his rounds, but there was nobody to check up on him at this hour of the morning. He checked the sound stages as he came to them. At Stage 23, he was surprised to find the door unlocked.

Wilbur entered the door and headed for the lighted area where the living room set was located. Someone must have forgotten to turn off the lights. When he saw the blood smeared on the bay window overlooking the painted harbor, he at first thought it was stage blood put there for a scene to be filmed later in the day. But when he touched the stain he found it still wet. It was then that he saw the body. He took it for a prop dummy until he touched it gingerly with his foot and saw the pool of real blood beneath it. The hairs on the back of his neck stood up, and he backed all the way to the exit.

Wilbur raced back to the office in his golf cart and called the police. It was the turn-around hour between the night shift and the day shift and it took a moment for the Day Watch sergeant to answer the phone.

"It's Wilbur Cross," stuttered the studio guard. He himself had wanted to be a real cop and had cultivated friends at the department.

"What's going on, Wilbur?" asked Phil Brownley.

"Murder," said Wilbur, taking some satisfaction in the drama he knew his pronouncement would make. He had never dreamed he would be a party to such a major crime.

"How do you know it's murder and who's dead?" asked the sergeant.

"You'd better get over here," Wilbur said. "There's a dead body on Stage 23 and I don't think she cut her own throat."

"We'll be right there," the sergeant said and hung up the phone.

Max Porter woke to the ringing of the phone. He rose on one elbow and looked out the large window overlooking Malibu Beach and the Pacific Ocean lapping quietly at the sand.

He had been dreaming of the new show he hoped to sell to the network and had a moment of anxiety when all the rich elements he had created in his dream were drained from memory.

Max Porter had been born in Brooklyn into a family whose income was derived from any number of illicit enterprises. He first entered show business as a member of a small traveling tent show. His specialty, which he had learned on the road, was as a barker inducing customers to pay to see such "freaks" as the bearded lady and the "geek" from Borneo who ate live chickens. The experience had served him well when he drifted into the wonderful world of television. He was still a huckster pitching half-truths to audiences to induce them to buy products they didn't need, couldn't afford, and in some cases, like cigarettes, could even kill them.

He looked at the woman on the pillow beside him. Most women he took for granted, but he could never get over his good fortune in finding Elena Gomez. He liked the fact that she was a full-bodied woman. While she slept, the sheet had slipped to reveal her ample breasts. Her nipples were brown and large and he savored the memory of the night before. He was fond of reminding himself that after all those greedy wives he had married and divorced, he was one lucky son of a bitch to have found her, like the Holy Grail, right next door.

She had come to him as a housekeeper, hired by his business manager. She lived in the servants quarters. He knew nothing about her and had paid her little attention until one night he came home unexpectedly and found her in the hot tub having a glass of his best chardonnay. He joined her in the hot tub. She started to leave, but he insisted she stay.

Since that night she had been not only his housekeeper but his bed partner. The relationship extended no farther than the beach house, and she had not pressed him, at first, to make her a more visible companion socially. But lately, as their relationship had become closer and, she thought, more meaningful to him, she had suggested they appear in public together. So far, he had avoided doing so.

The caller was Wilbur Cross from Magnum's Security department.

"Shit," Max said into the phone. "Any idea who did it?"

"Not yet," Wilbur said, "but we're working on it."

"Who is this broad, anyway, and what was she doing on my set?"

"We're working on it," Wilbur replied.

"Well, work harder," Max said. "And let me know what's going on." He slammed down the phone.

"What was that?" Elena asked. She raised one arm lazily and stroked his furry chest.

"Studio," Max answered, rising from the bed and tying the strings of his pajamas. "They can't wait to fuck up my day."

"What are they doing to you now?" she asked.

"They're killing people on my set."

"Is it someone famous?" If he had any dissatisfaction with Elena, it was her naive fascination with the movie stars he hired, fired and despised.

"Some so-called actress nobody knows. They'll know her now. It's going to hit the papers. I'd better get hold of publicity before somebody else puts the wrong spin on the story."

Emory Goode was doing push ups and watching the "Today" show when the phone rang. It was Max Porter informing him of the death of a woman on the set.

"It happened during the night," Porter said. "Nobody knows who she was or what she was doing there."

"Unless I miss my guess, I know. It's probably Lyla Taylor," Emory said after a long, somber moment. "I took her to the set. She was the girl we were going to audition today with Ariel Smart. I can't believe this."

"Are you crazy, Emory? What do you mean taking a broad on

my set? If you'd wanted a piece of ass why didn't you take her to your place?"

"It was nothing like that, Max. I gave her a little coaching, that's all."

"Is that what they're calling it these days?" Max said sarcastically.

"Just get off it, Max. I swear there was nothing to it."

"Well, you'd better get over to the studio and clear your story with the cops. But the important thing is to line up whatever scenes we can to shoot today. I'm not going to lose a day's work over this thing."

Emory returned the phone to the hook. Lyla was a calculating, scheming little baggage, but at the same time it was hard to realize she might be dead.

CHAPTER FOUR

The murder scene had already been secured by a uniformed officer by the time the two detectives from Homicide arrived—Pat O'Collins, a burly man in his fifties, and his partner Lana Slocum, a black woman in her late forties.

O'Collins was of medium height, dressed in a suit jacket with no tie. His reddish hair topped a round face with full cheeks and a flushed complexion. His bright green eyes, when they twinkled, tended to conceal his intelligence and his frank appraisal of a situation. People were inclined to like him at first sight.

Pat could not remember exactly when it happened, but at some point he had come to the realization that he was a middle-aged bachelor. He had always expected to marry, but somehow time had slid by, and he had spent all of his energy and days in being a good cop.

O'Collins had left the force in New York to come out to Hollywood as a technical adviser on a film based on a case he had solved. After that job was over, he had been hired for additional work on several films, but that had been twenty years ago. When the film work ran out he applied to join and was hired by the Los Angeles Police Department.

Lana Slocum was uncommonly tall, with light-colored skin and engaging chestnut eyes. She smiled often and had the gift of relieving tense situations with her sense of humor.

Lana had found the love of her life in Paul Slocum, a promising young police officer. They had been married only six weeks when he was shot and killed while foiling an attempted robbery at a liquor store in Korea Town. She never remarried and she satisfied the yearning for the children she could not have herself by adopting every child she could afford. To help her care for them, her mother had come to live with her.

On Stage 23, the Crime Scene Unit was already at work. Photographs and fingerprints had been taken and the area had been given a cursory search for evidence.

"So what happened here?" Pat asked the young officer who had been in charge until he arrived.

"Murder weapon looks to be a knife. It's been dusted for prints, but the technician thinks it was wiped clean before it was thrown away. It's been sent to the lab. Do you want to see the body?"

"No, not just yet," Pat said. "Let's take a look around while the scene is still fresh."

Pat and Lana used their flashlights to peer behind stage props and backdrops painted with views of city skylines or scenes of country meadows.

Finding nothing of interest, the detectives returned to the young officer in charge of the crime scene.

"Anything else before we go?" Pat asked. "Anything out of the ordinary that you know of?"

The young officer hesitated. "I don't know what to make of it, but the guard at Gate 4 reported that he saw Bette Davis drive off the lot during the night."

"I thought she was dead," Lana said.

"She is," said the young officer. "I probably shouldn't have bothered repeating it."

"We'll follow up on it," Pat said.

Once they had asked the routine questions Pat and Lana examined the body. The victim had been slashed several times across the face and her throat had been cut. They were accustomed to viewing dead bodies, but the shock of it, especially when the victim was young and beautiful, never wore off.

"What do you think?" Pat asked his partner.

"Not a professional job," she replied. "Looks like it was done by an amateur. He must have left the scene covered with blood."

"Took some strength to cut that deep."

"We'd better look into the men in her life."

"Get a list of the people who were on the lot last night," Pat ordered the young cop.

"It's already being done," he said.

"Any idea who she is? Was?"

"Name's Lyla Taylor. We found a purse with some identification inside."

"And find out where the production office is. I'd better let them know there won't be any shooting on this stage today. And we'd better find out what they know about the deceased."

Leaving the sound stage, Pat O'Collins breathed a deep sigh.

"Tired, partner?" asked Lana.

"You betcha," said Pat. He was tired. He was tired of murder and death. Even the challenge of solving a murder had lost some of the thrill it had once held for him. He wanted no more of it. He wanted to get back home. He wanted to spend a day at Montauk surf casting for blues. He wanted to have a long breakfast at the Stage Deli. And he wouldn't admit it, but it would be refreshing just once more to sit in the Radio City Music Hall and watch those long, dancing legs.

When permission was given to move the body, the two detectives watched while the shrouded body of Lyla Taylor was trundled on its gurney to the waiting vehicle to be transferred to the police morgue.

A small crowd had gathered at the edge of the yellow police tape that surrounded the sound stage. Technicians, film editors, secretaries, tourists and extras had come and gone, but a small core of the curious still lingered.

At the Gate 4 guard shack the young uniformed guard regarded them sheepishly when they questioned him about his sighting of Bette Davis.

"Isn't she dead?" Lana asked.

"I didn't say it was her," the young man objected. "I said it looked like her."

"Have you ever seen this person before?" Pat inquired.

"No," the guard said. "You see all kinds of kooks when you work this gate. After a while you don't pay that much attention."

"Didn't you stop her as she was checking out? Isn't that the routine?"

"She drove through without stopping," the guard replied.

"What kind of car was she driving? Did you get a license?"

The guard replied that he had not. He seemed less and less certain of the whole incident.

"I'll tell you the truth," the guard finally admitted. "I kind of dozed off there for a minute and it happened so fast I couldn't swear to it under oath."

"If you see her again, we'll want to talk with her," Pat said.

"Sure," the guard replied.

"Anything else you want to check out here?" Detective O'Collins asked his partner.

"Let's go by the production office," she answered.

CHAPTER FIVE

A riel Smart stopped her car at the Guard Gate. "I'm auditioning for *King's Harbor*," she said.

The guard consulted a list on the clipboard and at the same time gave her a thorough if discreet going over. Her blonde hair was held in a bun at the back of her head and her throat curved gently down to where the curve of her breasts began. She was an altogether gorgeous young woman, and to make her appearance perfect she seemed completely unaware of her beauty and its effect on her beholder. When she smiled, the guard's heart beat a little faster.

Reluctant to see her go, he directed her toward the make-up trailer.

She arrived at the make-up trailer to find Faye Nichols waiting for her. Faye was a good advertisement for her profession as a make-up artist. She seemed almost assembled from different body parts. Her hair was a lacquered helmet. Her fingernails were remarkably long and painted a rich vermilion. Her lipstick matched the fingernails. Her figure, thanks to a recently acquired ab machine, was trim and attractive. She did not look her fifty years.

"You've got a lot of work to do on me today," said Ariel. "I've been in San Francisco all weekend with my AHH group. I just came in from the Burbank airport."

"AHH. What's that?"

"It's a new group." said Ariel taking her seat in the director's chair that served the person being worked on.

"I first started working with them back in New York. Actors Helping the Homeless. We feed them and help them find jobs."

"Are you people having any luck doing that?"

"It's new out here, but in New York they're getting some good things done."

"I'm not even sure the audition is on for today," Faye said, "but I'll get you ready just in case." She began looking through her case of combs, selected one, and began work on Ariel's hair.

"Why wouldn't we do the audition?" Ariel asked.

"Listen, honey, I've got some terrible news. Have you heard any news reports this morning?"

"No, why?"

"Were you a friend of Lyla Taylor's?"

"I just met her one time in New York."

"Well, you don't have to worry about getting the part now. It looks like you don't have any competition."

"Did Lyla get a job on another show?"

"Lyla got her throat cut."

Ariel rose out of the chair and looked at Faye in astonishment and horror.

"Tell me this is just a joke."

"I wish it were. She was killed on the set. Security found her early this morning. The lot is swarming with cops."

Ariel felt ill. She had never before known a person who had been murdered. Back in Athens, Ohio, her hometown, the closest she had ever come to violence had been a fistfight between two students in a restaurant. And now she stood to gain a role because her competition had been murdered.

"I wanted this role, but I sure didn't want it handed to me this way," Ariel said. "Oh, that poor girl. She seemed a little tarty but . . . my God, murdered?"

★ ★ ★

The secretary had not yet arrived when the two detectives walked into the *King's Harbor* production office.

"Anybody here?" called Pat O'Collins.

His partner walked farther into the office.

"There's somebody back there," she said and pointed toward the row of office doors that stretched off down the corridor.

When they came to the source of the sound they found Justin Hargreaves busily at work in his office. He was obviously not expecting anyone and was startled by their appearance.

"Can I help you?" he asked.

Pat flashed his identification. "Detective O'Collins," he said.

"Anything wrong?" asked Justin. The several unpaid traffic tickets piled up on the dashboard of his car flashed through his mind.

"Who are you?" demanded O'Collins.

"Justin Hargreaves. I'm the writer on the show. And the creator," he couldn't help adding.

"I thought that the Man Upstairs was the Creator," said Lana.

"It's just a term we use in TV," the writer said, not amused. "Can I help you folks?"

"How long have you been here?" Lana asked.

"I started work last January."

"I mean here, today, at the studio."

"I don't know. I didn't look at the clock when I got here. I always come in early because I like to get to work on the script before it gets so crazy around here."

"Were you here last night?"

"Yes."

"How late?"

"I can't remember. I left some time after the fire."

"Did you notice what time you got home?"

"I didn't look at the clock. I just fell into bed."

"When you got here this morning," Lana said, "did you notice anything suspicious? Anything out of the usual when you came in."

"Did you see anybody near Stage 23? Anybody who shouldn't be around?" Pat added.

"No, the only person I saw was Emory Goode, the director. He stopped by at one point. What's all this about? Has this got something to do with that fire last night?"

"We're just checking around."

"Was anybody else here with you last night?"

"No."

"Is anybody else here with you this morning?"

"Usually the secretary's the next one in after me, but she's not here yet. I wish you'd tell me what's going on."

A door opened and closed down the hall. When footsteps came toward them they turned to see a tall, impressive figure entering. The two detectives turned to face him.

"Morning, Emory," Justin said.

"Howdy, folks. I'm Emory Goode."

"They're detectives," Justin explained.

"Is this about the murder then?" Emory said.

Justin looked at him questioningly. "What murder?" he asked.

"It was on the radio. Lyla Taylor was killed last night." Emory turned back to the detectives, and said, "I knew her. I was with her last night. Here on the lot."

"You might have been the last person to see her alive."

"That could be," Emory said. He looked to Justin and remembered that the writer had been here after he left and that Justin had been upset and threatening. An uncomfortable thought also came to him. Justin had been in a rage about Lyla's being cast as Tiffany. Was it possible that he had found a way to make sure Ariel Smart got the role?

"Do you have a suspect?" Emory asked.

"Until we find the killer, everybody's a suspect," Pat O'Collins replied.

CHAPTER SIX

I n the car, Lana took the wheel. The smog hung heavily over the basin, filling the air with its acrid, poisonous fumes. The sun shone through the smog as if through a filter and even at this early hour the temperature was reaching toward 80 degrees. It was a typical Los Angeles spring day.

"You can look out the window and enjoy yourself," she said to Pat. "We'll take the scenic route."

"That lets out Ventura Boulevard," Pat said, settling back in his seat.

"Do you know another way to get to Laurel Canyon?"

Once they had passed the attractive and substantial residences of Toluca Lake, past the homes of such stars as Bob Hope, Jonathan Winters, and Andy Griffith, they came to the more commercial area of the San Fernando Valley.

They turned right on Ventura Boulevard and made their way through the tawdry avenue of automobile repair shops, pizza joints, cheap Thai restaurants, tattoo parlors and nail emporiums.

On one corner an old homeless woman wearing a straw hat leaned on her shopping cart while she perused an old copy of *Vogue*. A dirty old mutt was asleep on a blanket in the cart.

"One cold winter night I stopped and gave that old woman a sleeping bag," Lana said. "I'd bought it especially because I felt sorry for her. She looked at it, felt it for quality, then handed it back and said, 'I've already got a better one.'"

O'Collins, his mind already on their destination in Laurel Canyon, smiled absently.

"Know anything useful about this dead girl before we get there?"

"Early twenties. Had an acting job here and there. Worked on the New York stage before she came out here. Might have worked the street briefly when she first came to town. No family that we've been able to find so far. We think she came from Canada, but we're checking that out."

At the top of Mulholland Drive Lana turned the car down Laurel Canyon, the steep mountain pass that separated Hollywood from the San Fernando Valley. When the rains were heavy it was impassable, and sometimes parked cars got washed down the canyon with the other debris. From somewhere came the distant aroma of a brush fire drifting into the car.

"Anywhere near us?" asked Lana.

"Not yet," said her partner, "but it will be if we don't move on. Did I ever tell you I once lived in Laurel Canyon?"

"Was that back in your hippie days?

"Those were before my time. No, this was when I was with that Creole girl and we thought we were in love. Turned out I was in love. She wasn't. She married some other man and moved to the Simi Valley."

Lana had been searching for addresses as they descended the curving canyon road. Three empty houses hung perilously over the side of the canyon. They had been abandoned after the last earthquake, a sad reminder of the uncertain stability of the earth's crust in Los Angeles.

"Could that be it?" Lana said, pointing to a box-like building of glass and redwood.

"Address is right," agreed Pat.

Lana stopped the car, parked and they went to the door. They listened for a moment to a Benny Goodman clarinet solo that came from somewhere deep within the house.

Pat rang the bell.

The doorbell was answered almost immediately by a man in his late twenties. He was bare-chested, wearing jeans and no shoes. His slim, muscular torso was obviously a source of pride to him.

"We're detectives Slocum and O'Collins." Pat announced. "We're investigating the death of Lyla Taylor."

"I'm her husband," he said. "I've been waiting for you to show up. I can't get an answer out of anybody about what really happened."

"What kind of answer are you looking for?" Pat asked.

"All I know is my wife's dead. I don't know where she is or how it happened. I want some answers."

Pat appraised the man by the open door. He didn't look like a man who would murder, but experience had taught him that anybody can kill if the circumstances are right.

"Can we come in?" Pat asked.

"Oh, sure. Name's David Taylor."

Both detectives, from habit and long training, took in the entrance and living room with a single glance. It was furnished in sleek, Danish furniture. An outsized nude painting of Lyla hung over the severely modern mantel.

"Any idea who could have killed your wife?" Lana asked.

"Not a clue."

"Anything you can tell us about her behavior lately?" Lana asked. "Has she been behaving strangely, anything out of the ordinary?"

"Just this part she's been trying out for. It's been the only thing she thought or talked about."

"Any friends? Anybody she's had an argument with recently?"

"Not that I know of."

"You mind if we take a look around?"

"What are you looking for? What do you expect to find?" he asked suspiciously. Lana wondered if he had something to hide.

"The bedroom through here?"

"Sure, go ahead." He seemed reluctant, but he let them proceed.

An unmade waterbed occupied most of the center of the room. A smoked mirror covered the entire ceiling.

Lana and Pat exchanged a meaningful look. The husband followed them into the room.

"You'll have to forgive me," he said. "I'm kind of in shock from all this."

"How long were the two of you married?" Pat asked.

"It would have been three years next month. That's us there," he said, pointing to a framed photograph on the bureau. It showed nice-looking younger versions of Lyla and her husband, smiling, standing in front of a car decorated with a Just Married sign.

"Where were you last night?"

"I was here," replied David. "Why do you want to know? You don't think I had anything to do with it, I hope."

"We have to ask these things," Lana answered. "So you were here. Was anyone with you?"

"No, I stayed up waiting for her. Watched television till I fell asleep."

"Weren't you worried when she didn't come home?"

He hesitated. "Sometimes, now and then, she would stay out all night."

"What would she be doing out all night?"

"You know show business. Sometimes you have to 'be cooperative' if you want to get ahead."

"Did she have any enemies? Anybody who might want to do this to her?"

"Everybody loved Lyla."

"Does the name Freddie Fine mean anything to you? We have reason to believe they knew each other."

For a moment the man's face flushed, but he quickly regained his composure. "I never heard the name."

Pat made a mental note that the man was lying.

"She had her life, and I had mine."

"What does that mean?" Lana asked.

"Nothing much. We were close. We just didn't tell each other every little detail of our lives. Maybe that guy was somebody she knew."

"What do you do for a living?" Pat asked.

"Clarinet. Clubs a lot of the time. Sometimes I get a call for work at the studio. I just did some background on that new Harrison Ford flick."

"Did she have any other relatives besides you?"

"She's got a sister, lives in Las Vegas. They used to do an exotic dancing act together. When her sister got married it broke up the act. The sister got out of the business, got married, had children. I sure hate to break this news to her."

"We'll do it," said O'Collins. "Just give us her address. We'll want to talk to her anyway."

"Listen, I guess I've got to make some arrangements. You know, funeral, some kind of service."

"All of that, and there's another thing you have to do. We need a positive identification of the body. You'll have to come down to the morgue with us."

"I'm not sure I can handle that."

"You'll have to."

CHAPTER SEVEN

Emory had been walking around the studio scouting for the right location to film one of his scenes. The studio really belonged on the National Register of Historic Places. So many of the old classics had been made here. Everywhere he looked he recognized backgrounds that had been used by other directors in the past, and the ghosts of such stars as Gary Cooper, Merle Oberon, John Wayne and Greer Garson were still lurking there in the shadowy sets.

He stopped by a Midwestern town square. From the front, the square was an idyllic representation of midtown America. The bandstand needed only a uniformed conductor in front of a brass band to burst into life and a Sousa March. On the porch of one Victorian house a swing moved gently in the breeze, and real birds nested in the branches of cardboard trees.

Emory walked only a few steps and observed that it was all a false front. From behind all that Midwestern innocence were the shabby backs of painted sets. The curtains that hung from the windows were tattered and grimy rags.

"I mustn't stay here long," he said to himself. "This town is a trap."

He knew the city well enough to recognize that the movie set was symbolic of the lives most Hollywood people led. It was all false, all a dream, for some a nightmare. Only a few of them ever woke from the dream long enough to be dismayed. A few others, a very few, woke in time to recognize that it was a nightmare and fled for their lives.

Emory walked on toward his lunch with Justin Hargreaves.

Hargreaves was sitting alone in one of the coveted booths in the studio executive dining room. When he had first come to the studio as a freelance writer, he'd had to wait in line for a table in the commissary. He'd come a long way. Why wasn't he happier?

He glanced around the room, which was beginning to fill with the lunch crowd. Executives who had never read a book in their lives were dictating their creative decisions to secretaries who trailed along behind them, only to be dismissed with a wave of their hands once they reached their tables.

Polly Goodman sat at one table holding court to a group involved in her newest picture. She was an ugly woman with a gray crew cut, dressed in her ubiquitous denim jackets and slacks. Forgotten were her several climbs and falls in the industry. She had used blackmail, the double-cross, sex and arrogance in her various climbs to the top. At the moment her latest picture was grossing enough to put her on top again. Justin thought of the manuscript of his novel. While it was not his main preoccupation, he did pull it out and work on it from time to time. He wondered if he might somehow get Polly to read it. She was "bankable."

Emory stopped at several tables to exchange greetings before he finally came to the booth where Justin waited.

"Sorry I'm late," he said. He laid his copy of the *King's Harbor* script next to Justin. "I've suggested some changes. Why don't you look them over?"

Justin was sullen and uncooperative, still smarting from the encounter he and Emory had had the night before.

"Whatever you say, boss," he said in a mocking tone.

"I know how you feel about me, Justin, but we do have to work together, and I'll meet you half way."

"Fine with me, just don't dictate what you want all the time.

It's my show, too."

"What we have to work out are some emergency scenes in case we get a fast go-ahead to start filming."

"Who do you think killed her?" the writer asked.

"Did you do it?" Emory asked.

"You are out of line!" Justin said. "Why would I even want the girl dead?"

"You were pretty upset last night about my casting her. And you did have the opportunity. You were still here when I left."

"How about you, Mr. Director? I don't know where you went after you left me. Maybe you went back and finished her off yourself."

"There isn't any actress that a director sooner or later doesn't want to kill, but this is silly. I wanted her for the role. Now, let's get to work."

The waiter came to the table carrying a phone. Emory hoped it was not for him. There was enough going on in his life without any more distractions. The dining room was filled, every table occupied with producers, writers, and other directors and executives. The "little people," those without reservations and those who could not get them, were lined up at the entrance.

The waiter plugged in the phone and handed it to Emory.

"It's Roberta," his wife said. "I've got to see you."

"I'm at lunch. How about this evening? Can't this wait?"

"It's about your daughter," she answered. When the phone went dead, Emory realized that she had hung up on him.

He turned to Justin Hargreaves.

"Excuse me," he said. "I've got to go."

"What about the scene changes? We've got to discuss them."

Emory set aside the script the two of them had been studying and with his napkin whisked away a crumb of bread that had fallen on his neat, well-creased trousers.

"What you showed me is fine," Emory answered, rising from the table. Many eyes followed him out of the dining room and many whispered comments that he had been the last person to see Lyla Taylor alive. He seemed totally unaware of the stares and whispers.

The sign in the directory of the Crescent Drive building in Beverly Hills read: Roberta Goode, Landscape Architect. Emory pushed the elevator button marked PH. The elevator rose briskly to the penthouse office.

Roberta functioned without a secretary, using instead a young horticulture student. It was he who admitted Emory to the apartment.

"I just spoke to my wife. She's expecting me."

Emory found Roberta at her desk, looking out over the green hills above the residential section.

He never failed to feel excited just by being in her presence. Even when they had quarreled before the separation, and the quarrels had become increasingly bitter and frequent, he had always felt an electricity radiating from her.

She was trim and elegant, imbuing even the plainest clothes with her inimitable style. Her hair was a rich russet and her brown eyes, set in her gently tapering face, were piercing yet friendly.

One of the things that had always amused Emory about her was that she found no satisfaction in working with plants unless she worked in the earth itself with her bare hands. No amount of skin lotion could conceal that this elegant woman had the hands of a toiler in the soil. The worry lines on her face told him that she had called about a serious matter.

Their separation had been years in coming. When it finally happened, he was directing a play in London. She was not a complainer, but she had come as close to complaining as she ever had just before he left New York.

"I'm tired of being a widow," she had said, and he had not

even heard her, so involved was he with the play he was going to be working on. He had invited her to London but she had declined. She and their daughter would be as abandoned in London as they were in New York. She was unwilling to make further excuses to their daughter for his absence from significant events in her life, such as parents' weekend at summer camp, or having her appendix removed.

Roberta had made excuses as long as she could, but on that particular absence she had gone back to her native California, taking their daughter with her, and opened an office to do what she most loved, to garden and design landscapes for others.

"I hear you're involved in something weird going on at the studio." She rose and took a step toward him. Since the separation they were momentarily awkward when they greeted each other. At times they would be on the verge of a handshake which more often than not culminated in a chaste peck on the cheek.

"A girl's been murdered. I was the last one to see her alive."

"Are you a suspect?"

"I shouldn't be, but I probably am. You called me about Robin. Is she all right?"

"I don't know. Have you heard from her?"

"She left a message on my machine a week or so ago, but when I called back there was no answer."

"She hasn't been home the last two days. Left no message and hasn't been to school."

"I wish you had let me know sooner," he said, hoping not to evoke a quarrel, but at the same time feeling irritated that they were unable to communicate.

"I knew you were starting a new show, and you'd be wrapped up in it."

It was the same note they had played most of the last year before they separated. He decided not to play it now, and asked, "Shouldn't we call the police?"

"She's done this before," Roberta said, "and she's always furious when she finds out we've notified the police. But she's never stayed away this long before. This time I'm really worried."

"Is she still doing drugs?" He hated the way the words sounded but could think of no other way to ask the question.

"I don't think she's ever stopped. She makes believe, but I'm not convinced."

"Have you any idea where she might be?"

"The only thing I found in her room was this matchbook."

She handed it to him with a look of ineffable sorrow and regret. The cover showed an address on Hollywood Boulevard and the name of a club spelled out in flaming red letters: *Hell*.

CHAPTER EIGHT

Marty Miller had never been to the City of Angels Country Club before and he felt silly as hell. With a towel wrapped around his scrawny waist he made his way through the steam-filled room.

He stopped when he came to a slab where a prone figure was being worked over by a Swedish Amazon with close-cropped hair. She was murmuring something in Swedish to the prostrate body while her client moaned with pleasure.

"Is that you, Max?" called Marty.

"Get out of here."

It was not the man he was looking for so Marty ventured on to the next cubicle.

"Max?" he called.

"Come on in, Marty," called Max.

Marty entered and found Max Porter being massaged by a tiny Oriental masseuse. She acknowledged Marty with a brisk nod then returned to pounding Max's back with the heels of her hands. The scent of coconut oil permeated the cubicle. Max, on his stomach, was nude except for a towel draped across his buttocks. Marty hadn't seen many naked men in his life; he was astonished by the amount of hair that covered Max's arms and back.

"Listen Marty, I've got twenty minutes I can give you. If we can't make a deal, I'll have to move on to the second choice. How much do you want for your girl?"

"You mean Ariel Smart?"

"Whatever her name is. She's not anywhere near being a star yet, so I'm not going to let you break my budget. I can offer scale for the first thirteen shows, see if she can cut the mustard, and after that we can talk about a ten percent raise."

In negotiations like this, Max knew it was best to take an aggressive position from the start. He could bully Marty Miller and make the deal he wanted to make. Agents like Miller disgusted him. He'd much rather deal with agents with more power and brains.

"Come on, Max. You and I have been in this business too long to start negotiations this way. You know you want my client, and you know she'll be good for the show."

"Little lower down, Mioki," Max said to the masseuse.

"Where were we?" Max said, looking back to the agent. He knew full well where they were.

"Not getting very far," Marty said.

"Listen, Marty, I know you're in debt up to your ass. You haven't got a client worth shit except for this little girl I'm trying to give a break to, and this deal can turn you around. Now, let's get down to some real business. Scale or no?"

"No," said the agent.

"Then make me an offer so I can let Mioki get on with my rubdown."

"I can go with two thousand an episode for thirteen if we're assured of five for the next order from the network."

"I'm on a tight budget."

"Then you make me an offer."

The banter continued for a full twenty minutes. Marty got nothing near what he wanted. Reality and the pressure of time forced him to close the deal on Max's terms. True, it was a steam room, but at the end Marty was sweating more than he should have been.

They shook to seal the bargain.

Marty, nervous, said, "We'll have to put this in writing pretty soon."

"My word's my bond," Max answered.

"That's what worries me," he replied unhappily. Max laughed.

"Have your girl on the set tomorrow at six o'clock," Max called as he turned back to the masseuse. Marty walked off through the steam and called back, "Will do."

In her recurring dream, Robin Goode was reliving the nightmare all over again. She was at home alone and she had let the boy come in because she trusted him. He had been more like a brother than a suitor.

They were listening to a Beatles recording when he put his arm around her. When she drew away she saw that his interest was not the least bit brotherly.

"I'm going to make love to you," he said.

"Don't be silly," she replied. "We're just friends."

"Don't kid around. You've been wanting it for a long time."

"Ted, you're all mixed up. I want you to get out of here now."

But he reached for her and pinned her, struggling, to the bed.

"My father will kill you," she said. "He'll be home any minute."

He laughed. She had already mentioned that her parents would be out for the evening.

When he began tearing at her underpants she screamed, but he covered her mouth with one hand and fumbled with his trousers with the other.

When it was over, he rolled over to his side and said, "Now, that wasn't too bad, was it?"

She raised her hand to strike him, but he struck her first. She was looking up at him, waiting for the next blow to fall. She always woke at this same moment.

Coming out of the nightmare she saw another face. A purple-haired boy with silver studs in each of his ears and a diamond-like stone in the tip of his tongue which was visible when he spoke.

"Some trip," he observed. "Where were you?"

"I was looking for my father," she said. "He wasn't around."

She rose to her elbow on the filthy mattress and looked around the otherwise empty room. Her head was spinning, her eyes felt enlarged, and she had the feeling she was moving back and forth in time like a slowly played accordion.

"Have you got anything?" she asked Purple Hair.

"You're already high enough," he said.

"I've got to come down," she said.

"Then let's go to the club. We'll find something for you there," and he led the way down the rickety stairs.

Ariel felt a familiar sense of serenity when she turned off the freeway onto the broad, palm-lined avenue to her apartment in Manhattan Beach. Already she anticipated the soothing sound of the surf that would come in her bedroom window. Manhattan Beach was a community of flight attendants, young professionals, lifeguards, and up-and-coming business people who gravitated there for the sun, the beach and the lifestyle.

Ariel pulled into the underground garage of the apartment house and parked beside her roommate's BMW convertible. She was pleased to see that her roommate was home. She would not be alone, and probably there would be food. Her roommate wasn't a gourmet cook, but she enjoyed preparing food and had taken over the cooking when they first moved in together. Weight conscious, neither of them ate heavily.

They had furnished the apartment with inexpensive, well-designed pieces from Ikea. The furniture had a modern Danish feeling, and they had brightened the room even more with color-ful throw pillows. The filmy draperies allowed a cheerful amount of sun to illuminate the room. Klee and Matisse prints decorated the walls. Beyond the window was a view of the Pacific which never failed to thrill the Ohio-born actress.

Ariel stopped at the refrigerator and noted with pleasure that her roommate had already prepared a salad for their dinner. She closed the refrigerator door and went on down the hall to her roommate's bedroom.

She found Joanne Gordon in her room, curled up studying one of the many textbooks that lined the bookcase beside her desk. Joanne, in what time she had to spare from being a flight attendant, was working toward her degree in psychology. She intended to become a family therapist.

"I saw the salad," Ariel said. "Thanks."

"If you want a dessert, you'll have to make it yourself," Joanne said. She was long and lanky, with striking red hair piled on the top of her head with a few curls spilling over around her ears. She wore the small pearl earrings of the size permitted by the airline.

"How is the student?" asked Ariel.

"Got an exam tomorrow and have to leave right from the classroom for my Mexico City flight. I guess you got that job, right?"

"Yes, but not the way I wanted it. My competition was mur-dered."

"I heard," Joanne observed. "Gruesome."

"How did you hear about it?" Ariel asked. "Can I sit?"

"Sure," answered her roommate. "It's been all over the TV news. Have they found the killer?"

"They don't seem to have a clue yet. The cops are all over the studio, questioning everybody."

"Even you?"

"Not yet, but they probably will."

"You did have a motive, didn't you?"

"Do I look like a killer to you?"

"I thought everybody was a killer in your business."

"Not true. I hear there are two or three very fine and princi-pled people in the industry."

"That creep has been sitting out there watching the apart-ment again, looking up at the window." Ariel crossed to the win-dow and looked out. "Who is he anyway? Why is he watching you?"

"I have no idea, and who says he's watching me? Maybe it's you he's so interested in."

"Thanks for making me feel good."

"Maybe he's head of your fanclub." Joanne said. They both laughed.

"Get back to your books," Ariel said and walked into her own room. She knew her parents would be worried when they read about the murder. She'd give them a call and set their minds at ease.

CURTIS HUGHES' JOURNAL

Nobody knows what hell a fan goes through. You spend your life trying to help your star any way you can but if you get anywhere near her you get these fishy looks and they call security. Like tonight. I wasn't hurting a thing, just sitting there looking up at her window, and I think she spotted me. Next thing you know a cop came cruising by and wanted to know what I was doing there. I made up some kind of excuse which he bought, but I can't go back because now my face is known. If Ariel really knew me, and she will one day, she'd trust me and let me be a real close-up fan. In the meantime I will stay as close to her as I can. Little does the audience know that one person has already given her life for Ariel's career.

CHAPTER NINE

The International Broadcasting Company (IBC) started out in 1920 in the back room of an amateur inventor, Angus Walker, in Newark, New Jersey. From a crystal radio he had developed a device so sophisticated that music and voice could be clearly heard and transmitted over wide areas.

When Angus Walker died, his son developed the toy into a radio that was able to compete with Atwater-Kent and RCA. From manufacturing radios the son went into radio broadcasting, and his company grew into one of the major networks in the country. When television became commercially viable, IBC relegated radio to a secondary position and jumped with both feet into television.

Today it occupied a position equal to NBC and CBS and covered a full block of expensive real estate in Hollywood and a skyscraper in New York. Gerald Walker, descendant of the founding family, was ostensibly active in the management of the network as head of programming, but he was more interested in buying antiques and traveling than in the business.

From time to time Walker became caught in a situation which demanded a decision. This was such a time. Max Porter had called right at the end of the day and made an appointment for seven o'clock.

Gerald had held over his assistant and the casting director, since the assistant suggested that Max's problem probably had to do with the casting on *King's Harbor*.

Gerald's assistant, Sherwin Fields, was short, scrawny, and singularly unattractive. He came from a poor family in Bakersfield, California, and was determined to make something of himself. He determined early on that the broadcast industry provided a field where great income could be derived quickly with no great talent other than a good head on one's shoulders.

Fields had joined the network right out of the USC film school where he had graduated with honors. He had devoted himself to his immediate job, but his main course of study was climbing the corporate network ladder as quickly as possible. He feigned an avid interest in antiques, studied the magazines, informed himself about the field, and even managed to be seen at major antique shows by Gerald Walker.

Once he caught Walker's attention, he rose quickly through the ranks until Gerald had become content to allow him to make major decisions, often without even consulting with him. Sherwin's was a position of power and he was greatly feared. Many executives were waiting for him to fall, but so far he had remained quite nimble on his feet.

Gerald, in a yellow cashmere sweater, paced his office impatiently. He had an appointment with an antique dealer who had just received a container of pieces of rare eighteenth-century glass from Venice. He did not want to take a chance that some other collector might get there ahead of him. Gerald did not like picked-over treasures.

He was relieved when he saw Max and his writer drive into the parking lot below.

"They're here," he said to Sherwin Fields. "Put something on that Chippendale chair so Max doesn't sit on it. Remember the one he broke the last time he was here?"

In the parking lot, Porter parked his red Porsche in a space reserved for top executives. During regular hours these spaces would be filled with Mercedes and Jaguars, the vehicles of choice of most of the highly paid executives.

A long line of tourists and fans waited to be admitted to the taping of a game show.

"Assholes," Max observed of the people in line.

"They're our audience," chided Justin.

"Still assholes," he said.

They entered the lobby. As they were crossing the lobby the receptionist called, "Do you have a pass, sir?"

Max said, "I don't need a pass," and continued on to the locked door that led into the offices.

His way was blocked. The receptionist had failed to push the button that would unlock the door.

"Open the fucking door," he shouted, rattling the handle.

"You have to give me your name, sir, and tell me where you're going!"

"I'm Max Porter, and I'm going to see Jerry Walker, and what's your goddamned name, by the way, so I can mention to Jerry how courteous you've been."

"Tell him Eva let you in," she said. "And if he wants to fire me, it's okay by me!"

She released the lock. Max and Justin entered the office area.

"Where do these fucking people come from?" complained Max on the elevator.

"Calm down, Max," Justin said. "You'll scare the pants off Gerald, and we need his approval for this casting."

When they got off the elevator the floor had the hushed, deserted feeling left when all the workers had gone home for the night. A secretary came out of the executive suite and ushered them inside.

They entered the lavishly appointed corner office which Gerald Walker had furnished with his most precious Louis XIV pieces. Walker rose and shook hands with Max. Only after Justin reminded him that he had never met Gerald did Max introduce the writer.

Max was sorry to see that Sherwin Fields was at the meeting. He was a rattlesnake. Max had tried to get along with him for business reasons but had never succeeded in establishing any warmth or cooperation with the rising young executive. Sherwin greeted him with his usual slightly insincere smile.

Molly French, the network casting director, came forward and greeted them. The studious looking young man who sat outside of the inner circle with his pencil poised to take note of anything said or done was not introduced. This job was the training ground for young people with aspirations whose families had the proper connections. If he played his cards right he could easily become the next Sherwin Fields.

"I hear we lost Lyla," Molly said.

"You could put it that way, Molly," Justin said.

"That was the young woman we were considering for the role on *King's Harbor*?"

"Got a better one for ya," Max said. "Ariel Smart."

"She is good," Molly said. "I know her work."

Sherwin Fields said, "I think we should audition some more girls."

"Haven't got time for that," Max said.

"And besides," Justin said looking nervously at Max, "she's the best actress for the role." Max liked to do all the talking. He was simply there for window dressing. Max tried to keep Justin away from the network to prevent his learning how things worked and taking independent action that might lead him away from Max's grasp. Justin worried about Sherwin Fields, who was convinced that the way to high ratings were paved with chesty women wearing tight, wet T-shirts. His vision of Tiffany did not coincide with the kind of girl Sherwin was sure to try to cast.

Gerald looked at his watch. If he left now he could get to the warehouse in Long Beach before the other buyers.

Hoping to find an ally, Molly turned to Max and asked, "How does Emory feel about Ariel? I know when we first read her he felt she was a bit too ladylike."

"Emory's crazy about her," Max lied. "He was sorry he couldn't be here with the rest of us but some personal business came up."

Gerald asked, "Can we make a deal with this Ariel Smart?"

"Leave it to me," Max said, remembering with pleasure the tough bargain he'd already driven with her agent.

"I'd be more comfortable if we looked at some more actresses," said Sherwin.

"Ariel's right on the nose for the job," Justin said with a defiant look at Max, but Max nodded in agreement. He, too, wanted to start filming as quickly as possible so as not to lose money by waiting longer.

"Karen Dawson is free," Sherwin said. "The show she was in just got canceled at CBS. She could start work tomorrow."

"I hate Karen Dawson," Justin said. He knew as soon as the words were out of his mouth that he had spoken out of turn.

Sherwin said, "I love Karen Dawson. She's got just the quality the character needs."

"Hooker time," Justin said vehemently, red-faced.

"I say we cast Ariel," Max said.

Gerald snuck another look at his watch and said, "I trust Max. Let's go with his conviction."

"You're the boss, boss," Sherwin said, smiling at everyone in the room. "I'll get the paperwork rolling."

As they were leaving the building Justin, feeling elated that Ariel had gotten the job, said, "We did it, didn't we?"

"You almost blew it, kid. You talked too much," Max said. "Next time leave it all to me."

Emory pulled up to the address Roberta had given him. At first he thought he was at the wrong place. From the outside it looked like an abandoned warehouse, but after a moment a young man, limping slightly, wandered over casually, leaned in the open window and asked, "Are you lost, Mister Goode?"

"How do you know my name?"

"I've parked your car at other places."

"Have I found Hell?"

"Smack in the middle of it!"

"I want you to park my car, but I want it in a well-lighted place, I want it locked, and I want you not to take your eyes off it until I come back," Emory said, handing the boy a twenty.

"Don't worry about a thing."

Emory got out of the car and looked toward the building behind him.

"I don't see any entrance."

The boy said, "First door on the right down that alley," pointing the way. He was a handsome kid with an all-American look to him, but there was something in his eyes that worried Emory momentarily.

Emory felt the throbbing music even before he pushed aside the surprisingly heavy door. A tall blonde woman wearing a trim Versace suit looked him over carefully.

"Are you sure you're in the right place?" she asked. Her voice was deep and so masculine that he wondered for a moment if she was really a woman. In some of these nightclubs gender was difficult to determine.

"I think my daughter might come here. I'm trying to find her."

"Come in, but first Bruce would like to introduce you to our protocol."

She beckoned to a strapping young bruiser who patted Emory down from his head to the cuffs of his trousers. Emory decided not to resist and endured the invasion of his space stoically. The bouncer nodded, and Emory made his way toward the bar.

Passage was not easy. The room was packed with young people and some surprisingly not so young, all heavily made up in dark, bizarre patterns around their eyes, throats, and hair. Some wore the green and purple spiked hair that Emory had observed young boys and girls wearing on Hollywood Boulevard, but the predominant guise was macabre and vampirish.

A heavy cloud of smoke hung in the hot, heavy air, the sweetly nauseating aroma of marijuana mixed with resinous traces of hash, beer, sweat and whiskey.

On a raised platform in the corner, five girls made up like Charles Addams characters pounded various instruments. In a cage suspended from the ceiling in the middle of the room, a girl wrestled endlessly with a twenty-foot anaconda. Singles and couples writhed and swayed to the harsh beat of the heavy metal music. By the time he reached the bar, Emory wondered if his hearing had been permanently damaged.

The bartender had so many metal rings piercing his eyes, ears, nose, mouth and tongue that it was hard to know exactly what he looked like.

"Want a Shirley Temple, daddy?" asked the barkeep.

"Would you have a decent chardonnay?"

"Sure," said the young man, and pulled out an opaque bottle with no label on it.

Emory looked at the murky wine with distaste.

"What's your name?" asked Emory.

"Death," said the boy. "What's yours?"

"Life," said Emory.

It was then that he spotted Robin. She was dressed all in black and he realized why he had not recognized her immediately. Her face seemed caked with flour. Her eyes were outlined heavily in black and over her breast she wore a heart so real in appearance that it might have been removed from her chest cavity. The young man beside her was tall and thin and had purple hair.

As Emory forced his way through the crowded tables, chairs

and dancing couples, he saw Robin and the young man leave through the back door. It took him several minutes to reach the door. He stepped out into the alley. She was gone.

When the valet approached him, he asked, "Did you see a pretty young girl and a boy with purple hair just come out here?"

"I try not to see anything around here."

CHAPTER TEN

Ariel was dressed and waiting for the studio driver to pick her up for her first day's shooting. She tried to control her excitement as she stood looking out at the Pacific. It was one of those days when the ocean turned turquoise blue and sea green and rolled gently in over the sloping sand. Ariel thought of the long road she had taken to arrive at this point in her life. She thought of her parents who would just be getting out of bed back in Athens, Ohio. She thought ruefully of her younger brother who used to burst into her room when she stood in front of the mirror practicing a scene, of how she chased him through the house, hurling screams and curses. She thought how much she missed them all right now, but also how proud they would be when they saw her on *King's Harbor*.

"What's for breakfast?" Joanne asked as she stumbled through the living room on her way to the kitchen. Joanne was a heavy sleeper and claimed that often she was half-way through her first flight of the day before she woke up. This news did not comfort Ariel when she had to fly.

"I did make some coffee," said Ariel.

"No ham and eggs?"

"You can get that on your flight to Mexico City. When will you be back?"

"Scheduled for Thursday."

The doorbell sounded. "There's my driver," Ariel said.

"Break a leg," Joanne said.

The driver was an earnest young man who almost fell over himself to be helpful to Ariel.

"My name is Chuck. The car's downstairs."

Ariel followed the young man to the elevator and out onto the street. He held the door open for her, and she slid into her seat.

"Let me know if it's warm enough back there," he said over his shoulder. "These early California mornings get kind of chilly."

"Is there a light back here?" Ariel asked. "I want to look over my script one more time."

"That switch there by the window," Chuck said. "You're playing Tiffany, they tell me."

"I'm sorry about that other girl," Ariel said, glancing away from her script for the moment.

"I drove her once on another show. She was nice. Kind of hard to know, but seemed real serious about her work and all. She's with the Lord now, God bless her."

Ariel recognized that her driver was probably a born again Christian. It seemed an incongruous trait for a studio driver to have, but Ariel had ceased to wonder about anything in Hollywood.

Entering Gate 4, the security guard saluted and said, "Good morning, Miss Smart."

She hadn't even worked a day and already the security people knew her name! She had been driven to the studio like a star! She felt elated. She had arrived in Hollywood.

The three-story old Victorian in South Pasadena seemed to vibrate with life even before Pat O'Collins entered. He sounded the bell several times and realized that the din from children getting the day started probably prevented Lana or her mother from hearing the doorbell, so he turned the handle and entered the unlocked front door.

Children descended upon him from everywhere, yelling "Uncle Pat, candy, candy, candy!" Pat wondered how Lana had managed to keep such a wide ethnic range of children. They were white, black, red, brown and yellow. Some were adopted and others were foster children. They all treated Pat as their uncle, father, friend. He spent much of his free time with the children, taking them to the playground, ball games, and fishing in Macarthur Park.

Pat shook himself free, cuffed a couple of the boys, and said, "Now go get ready for school. Uncle Pat wants to say hello to your grandma."

He found Lana's mother in the kitchen smoking a cigarette. She was sitting directly beneath the No Smoking sign on the wall, surveying a pile of dirty dishes.

"If you want coffee," she said, "you'll have to wash your own cup. They've dirtied everything in the house, including the ceiling. How they get food up there I'll never know."

"It's an old trick. Done by flipping a spoon," Pat answered with a laugh, "Mind if I open the window? Your smoke is even more dangerous than eating here."

"Fine, as long as you don't let any of the kids sneak back in."

"Lana almost ready?" Pat asked, pouring coffee into one of the cleaner-looking cups.

"I think she's barricaded herself in her room while she puts on her make-up!"

"The barricade didn't work," Lana said as she walked in, waving her hands to clear the room of smoke. "If you weren't my mother, I'd throw you out of here," she said.

"If you bring any more children around here, I'll throw you out," Mabel Turner said.

"Let's go to work and get away from this cranky old woman," Lana said.

In the unmarked police car, Pat took the wheel.

"Want to drive to San Francisco?" he asked. Each morning

he asked her if she wanted to drive to some unlikely place such as Vancouver or Chicago. It had started as a joke but had become routine and boring. It was a habit he couldn't seem to break.

"Like to," she said, "but we'd better get to work."

Work for the day began with calling on one of the men whose checks they had found in Lyla Taylor's purse.

The address was in the factory section of Santa Monica. A billboard on top of the building proclaimed that this was the home of Superfine Fine Toys for Girls and Boys, Freddie Fine, Prop.

Freddie himself welcomed them into his richly furnished office. The chairs and sofas were elegant French antiques and blended tastefully with the modest credenza and bookcases. Nothing in the room suggested the home of a toy czar.

"I read about that girl," he said before they even had a chance to speak. "How did you find out about my connection to her?"

"We found your check," Pat said.

"Any chance of getting that back?" Freddie asked. "I'll be in deep trouble if my wife finds out about that."

"How well did you know Lyla Taylor?" Lana asked. "What was your relationship with her?"

"It was financial. You know, you've got my check. It was a mistake to pay with a check. I should have given her cash."

"What were you paying her for?" Pat asked.

"Well, she provided a service, and I paid for it."

"Are we talking about sex?" Pat asked.

"Sure, what else would I want from a woman like that?"

"Did you know she had a husband?"

"I met the husband. Some times she would come here, but once in a while we went to her place. Last time we did, the husband walked in on us."

"What was his reaction?"

"He knew what she did for a living. He lived off it."

x

"Have you seen him since?"

"Yes, he came here once."

"You want to talk about that?"

"Not especially, but you might as well know. He wanted money. Seems he had made a video of Lyla and me. Said he would send it to my wife unless I took care of him."

"What did you do?"

"I took care of him."

Everyone on Stage 23 was aware of the roped off living room set of *King's Harbor*. The yellow police tape was a gruesome reminder of the murder that had taken place only twenty-four hours ago, but as Max Porter reminded everyone, "This show must go on," by which he meant that he was not going to lose another dollar because of a small thing like a murder on his sound stage. Filming had been moved away from the scene of the murder to another part of the sound stage.

"This is a rehearsal," called Emory Goode. "First team up."

While the stand-ins retired from the positions they had held so the lighting could be adjusted and the director and camera-man could rehearse the next shot, Emory gave the set one final going over.

The scene was not an unusual one for a nighttime soap pilot. The character named Tiffany is opening an important letter from Rodney announcing that he knew she was thinking of selling *King's Harbor*, and that he would expose her past if she did. Emory watched the new actress, Ariel, approach with the make-up man still touching a wisp of hair and the costumer following behind her with critical tugs and pats at her dress.

Emory liked the fact that she appeared a little nervous. He could turn that nervousness into energy once the scene was underway.

When she reached her mark, Emory checked the bar beside

her to see that the knife she would use to open the envelope was in place. He had intentionally kept from the actress that a knife just like this one, and in the same position, had killed Lyla Taylor. Now he crossed to the area behind the camera where Max Porter and Justin Hargreaves were watching.

"Do you like the look?" Emory asked Porter. "Anything you want changed before I shoot it?"

"I like it," Porter said.

"And how about you?" he asked Hargreaves.

"I think she needs a little more color in her cheeks. She shouldn't look so pale."

"I'll tell make-up," Emory said.

As she began the scene, Ariel's nervousness fell away. She seemed oblivious to those who were watching the scene. She played to the camera as if she'd been doing it all her life, and even in rehearsal the performance was convincing, real and moving. She had become Tiffany.

The director called "Cut" and there was a smattering of applause.

"Not yet," Emory called. "Don't turn my actress's head. Let's wait for a take."

With the camera rolling, Ariel performed the scene, again to perfection.

"Print it," the director called and looked at the producer and the writer. They were both nodding and smiling.

"That girl is just what we need," Max said. "Exciting, sexy, and talented. Where did we find her, anyway?"

"I had seen her on *The Guiding Light*," Justin said, "suggested her to casting, and they brought her in."

"She's worth a million dollars," Max said.

"Shall I tell her that?" Hargreaves asked with a grin.

"Do, and I'll break both your kneecaps," Max said. "You guys stay here and jerk off. I've got work to do."

On his way out he stopped long enough to say to Ariel, "You

did good. Keep up the good work." He tried to pat her on her behind, but she shied away.

"Just don't ask for a raise," he said in parting.

She smiled after him. She knew the ropes. She knew that the actors on *Friends* had gone from $50,000 an episode to $100,000 an episode. This wasn't *Friends*, but it was the same game.

The director, too, stopped to see her when the day's work was finished.

"Your work was splendid today," he said.

"Did that surprise you?" she asked. There was a resentful edge to her voice.

"Not at all," he answered.

"Then why were you so against casting me in the first place?"

"I'm sorry you heard about that. It had nothing to do with your ability. I wanted Lyla because she had a natural, tramp-like quality where you have a natural ladylike quality. She would have done Tiffany without even trying. You have to act the part."

"I hope I didn't disappoint you."

"By no means. And I should tell you, there was one other reason."

"I'm listening."

"I guess I hated what might become of you if this pilot becomes a hit. There's something corrupting about fame and money, and I wouldn't want you to be changed by it."

"I'm an actress. That's a challenge, and I think I'm up to it."

"I hope so," he said. "At least now we've cleared the air, and we'll be friends."

"I'd like that," she said.

CHAPTER ELEVEN

Ariel was still on a high when she reached the end of the day's work.

"Everybody get a good night's sleep," Emory called. "I want you fresh and ready to go in the morning."

A good night's sleep was the last thing Ariel wanted. She didn't care if she never slept again. She had spent the day doing exactly what she had dreamed of doing from the time she was a little girl. She had done it well. She had been praised.

When Justin Hargreaves came by the set and invited her to have dinner with him, she accepted at once.

"We can talk about your character," he said, as though she needed any further persuasion.

"Have I got it right?" she asked anxiously.

"You can get it even more right if I tell you a little bit more of her background," Justin said.

Ariel had never been to the Chaya Brasserie before. There was no one over thirty in the restaurant. It was filled with young actors, writers, directors and lawyers.

The hubbub was so loud that on the way home she could recall little of what Justin Hargreaves had said to her. Not that it mattered much. She was still carried along on the wave of euphoria that had been building all day.

"You can just let me off in front of the building," she said.

"No way," he answered and pulled into an empty space. "I'm going to see you right to your door."

"I can't ask you in. I've got to be up at the crack of dawn."

"Never crossed my mind," he said. He came around and opened the door for her and they started for her apartment building.

On a park bench between the building and the boardwalk, a young man sat gazing intently up at the third-floor window. He sat back from the street light, half in shadow.

Ariel stopped and took Justin's arm.

"I think that's the creep who's been watching our apartment," she said. "I think he's the one who makes those scary phone calls to me in the middle of the night and hangs up."

"We'll see about that," Justin said. "You wait here."

"Don't you dare leave me alone," she said, and together they walked toward the man. He turned now, aware that they were approaching him.

"What are you doing?" Ariel called. "What do you want?"

The figure rose hurriedly and ran off with a slight limp. Within seconds he was out of sight.

It was nearly midnight and Emory was home and working late. He was elated over the way the first day's shooting had gone. He was especially pleased with the work Ariel had done. She was exciting to work with and, as all truly talented people do, she gave a new dimension to the scenes.

She had impressed him so favorably he was examining all the scenes he would shoot tomorrow to see how he might feature her talent.

He started to ignore the phone when it first rang. Wrong number, he decided. Nobody he knew would be disturbing him at this hour. And then he reasoned that there might be some problem with tomorrow's shoot and picked up the phone.

"Mr. Goode?" asked a gruff male voice.

"Yes?" he answered.

"This is Sergeant Thompson at the Hollywood Division. We have your daughter."

"Please explain," said Emory.

"Your daughter has been taken in for curfew violation. She gave us this number. We can release her into your custody. Otherwise she will remain here overnight."

"Could you give me an address, please?"

He scribbled the address on a notepad, dressed in a frenzy, and was still buttoning buttons when he ran out of the room.

Coming out of the Briarwood Apartments he turned left on Barham Boulevard and left again on Cahuenga. The city was silent, empty and ominous. There were so many dark places, with an odd mixture of city streets and country lanes. Even the freeway adjacent to Cahuenga seemed threatening, available for freeway shootings and random violence.

The areas in New York which were known to harbor criminals were easier to avoid. Here danger seemed all-pervasive, liable to reach out and grab you.

At the station he faced an officer sitting at a high desk just inside the entrance.

"I'm Emory Goode, here to pick up my daughter, Robin."

He could see through the grillwork when Robin was brought from the back of the station by another officer who handed her what Emory assumed were her possessions. The officer led her to the front of the room. The black makeup around her eyes had streaked from her tears, and the ghoulish heart she had worn earlier around her neck was still pulsing from its chain. She saw him and looked away.

"Let's go home," he said.

When she came forward, he tried to hug her but she shrugged him away.

"Are you all right?" he asked.

"Never better," she said.

A sharp, bitter rejoinder came to his mind. Did the girl have any idea of the agony she had caused her mother and him these recent weeks? But he held his tongue. He felt the agony she was going through, and this was no time to show anger.

He held the passenger door open for her.

"No thanks," she said and climbed into the back seat.

"I'd rather you'd sit up here," he said.

"You're not directing this show," she said.

They drove for a block in silence.

"Would you like to come home with me or would you rather go to your mother's?"

"The rest of my coven is out at the Veteran's Cemetery. You can drop me there, if you don't mind."

"I would mind very much," he said. "Robin, do you know that I love you?"

"Where were you when I needed you?" she said. "Thanks for springing me." They had arrived at a stoplight. She opened the backdoor of the car and before he could restrain her, she had faded off into the dark city.

CHAPTER TWELVE

The screening room was old, shabby and worn from years of impersonal use by writers, producers, editors and directors. Bowing to the current intolerance of smokers, the ash trays had been removed, but smudged spots on the floor bore testimony to a generation of viewers who had ground out cigarette butts with the heels while they looked at their dailies of yesterday's filming.

Just sitting near Ariel elated Justin Hargreaves. He was conscious of the perfume he had come to associate with her. He had asked her the name of it. "Paris." The whole experience was heightened by the illicit nature of it. Dailies were never supposed to be shown to members of the cast.

While waiting for the projectionist to arrive, Justin asked, "Was everything all right last night after I left you? Did you see the creep again?"

"I was a little nervous," she answered, "and I looked out the window a couple of times but didn't see him again."

"Have you any idea who he is?" Justin asked.

"Sometimes the phone rings and there's just heavy breathing," she answered.

"One of those," he said. "Do you carry anything, mace or a whistle so you can call for help?"

"No, but I guess I should. Let's not worry about it. Right now I'm more worried about these dailies."

"I think you're going to be pleased," he said. "But if anybody asks, you didn't see them. It's a cardinal sin in the industry to show dailies to actors."

"My lips are sealed," she said. "I'm curious and I want to ask you about my character. And I wonder if we think of her the same way. How do you envision Tiffany?"

"Very important to the plot. Important to the series. You haven't seen the story projection, but Tiffany will probably inherit *King's Harbor* when her father dies. She will then be the series lead."

"Wow," said Ariel eagerly. "Am I playing her to your satisfaction? What more can I give to the character?"

"I just want you to be comfortable with the role for the time being," Justin said. He actually did have some notions about how she should play the part, but he did not want to burden her with any negative thought at this moment. "We can work together when I'm ready to enlarge the role and she takes over in a more forceful way."

"Tell me, is the network happy with my work?"

"They are now. There was one executive who wanted Lyla Taylor. He thought she gave it a common quality that frankly you don't have and I don't want."

"Does that mean you don't find me sexy?" Ariel asked. She was immediately sorry. It sounded as if she were looking for a compliment.

"I find you extremely sexy, now that we've opened that door. Lyla was sexy, too, but the way a slut or a tramp might turn somebody on."

"I can bring that kind of physicality to it, if that's what you want," Ariel said. Again she hoped that he had taken her remark in a professional way and would not twist her meaning.

"I know," he said. "I've seen everything you've ever done, but right now you're playing Tiffany just the way I envision her."

"How did you ever get the concept for *King's Harbor* anyway? Have you ever lived down around Newport?

"Actually it's *Dallas* on the water. Haven't you noticed?"

"I didn't think you were one of those California surfers who grew up on sunshine and orange juice."

"Long way from it," he said. He wondered if she was as conscious of him as he was of her. He was almost afraid that in this semi-dark room he might forget himself and reach over and touch her beautiful throat. He had dreamed of being this close to her, and now that the moment was at hand he felt the excitement in his groin.

"Where did you grow up?" she asked.

"When we know each other better I'll tell you what it was like to grow up in a preacher's household in a little town in Minnesota."

"Was it good or bad?" she asked.

"Let's just say it was something I'll write about one of these days."

"Do you go back?" she asked. "Family still there?"

"Not anymore," he answered. He didn't want to tell anymore about his family.

Fortunately the projectionist arrived in the control room and said, "Ready when you are, Justin."

Justin pushed the audio button on the console beside his chair. "Roll the film," he said.

And then, turning to the beautiful girl beside him, he said, "Enjoy."

The lights dimmed.

When she saw herself on film, Ariel became completely professional and objective. She observed the make-up, the way she moved, and the hairdo. She made mental notes as to how best to direct those responsible for her appearance and make it even better.

In the scene on film she had just learned of the illness of her father. Tiffany loves her father deeply. The scene called for several emotions—love, anxiety, apprehension, surprise and shock. Both she and the writer were pleased with her performance.

"Like the young Hepburn," whispered Justin. "Coltish. Long-legged. Prancing!"

"Don't I wish!" said the actress.

They were so caught up in the scene that they were both startled when the door opened and someone glided into the room and took a seat in the row behind them.

"Who is that?" called Justin.

"I'm your director," Emory Goode said quietly but with an implied message that Justin picked up on.

Emory had the good manners to wait until the actress had made her exit before he expressed his displeasure with the writer.

"Okay," said Justin. "I was wrong, and I admit it. Did you see enough of the film to see how good she is?"

"She works. She can handle the part."

"But she's more right for the role than Lyla ever was."

"You're not going to get me to agree with you. Ariel will be fine. Lyla just never had a chance to show what she could do."

"I was right, and you'll eat your words yet."

"I'm not eating anything," Emory replied, "and now if you'll excuse me, I'm scheduled for this room to see my dailies by myself."

Justin left the room. Emory pressed the intercom and said, "Please, re-rack and roll the film again."

The gambling industry permeated every aspect of life in Las Vegas. O'Collins and Slocum had been to the city before and were not surprised at the number of slot machines that lined their way out of the airport. They took a taxi to the address David Taylor had given them.

The cocktail bar was called "The Cat House," and the aroma

of beer and cigarettes, the faint scent of perspiration and a curtain of blue smoke met Lana and Pat as they entered.

The bar ran the length of the long, dimly lit room. The endless whir of slot machine handles being pumped was punctuated with the regular grind of the levers and the occasional cry of delight and tinkle of coins when the cherries lined up together.

A big, beefy man who could have been a bouncer, an owner, or both, greeted them.

"A couple of slots open way in the back, folks," he said.

Lana and Pat smiled and flashed their IDs.

"We're just visiting," Lana said. "You have an employee named Millie Flowers working here?"

"What's the trouble?" the man asked.

"We just want to talk to her for a couple of minutes if you don't mind."

"Have a seat and I'll send her over," he said, trying to conceal the impatience he felt. Millie was one of his best waitresses and he did not want her out of circulation for long.

Passing a battery of slot machines, Pat jingled the coins in his pocket.

Lana said, "I know you're dying to, Pat, so why don't you throw away a quarter?"

"Just to get a feel of the place," he replied.

He put the quarter in the slot and pulled the handle. The mechanism whirred and came up with two cherries and a pear. He was reaching for another quarter when a woman approached.

She was dressed in black net stockings and her face was made up like one of the characters from the musical "Cats." Behind her was attached a long black tail motored by some mechanical device so that it swept from side to side provocatively as she walked.

"You wanted to see me?"

"Can you join us for a moment?" Lana asked.

"I'm serving right now, and the boss doesn't encourage sitting with customers. What do you people want? Is this about my sister?"

"Yes," replied Pat. "We're trying to find out who killed her. Have you any idea who might have done it?"

"My sister and I were not close. I don't know much about her life over there. We had a falling out."

"What kind of falling out?"

"Maybe you should ask her husband that."

"He said we should talk to you," Lana said.

"Might be better for you in the long run just to be open with us," Pat advised.

"I'll be open and I'll be quick. I make my living on tips, so the sooner we finish the better. What exactly can I tell you?"

"Whatever seems important to you."

"We came here from New York. She'd had a couple of acting parts there, but the work ran out. We decided to make a new start out here and do an act together. Exotic dancers. And we were doing okay until this musician came along."

"David Taylor?"

"That's the jerk. First she let him move into our extra room, and in no time at all he was in her bed. Said he was in love with her but tried to put the make on me when she wasn't around. Anyway, Lyla married him, and he started sucking every cent out of her he could. We had a joint bank account, planned some day to open a little place on the edge of the strip. And then one day the two of them just up and disappeared. First I learned of what they'd done was when I tried to cash a check. 'Out of funds' they told me at the bank. My sister and that asshole had ripped me off."

"You must have been mad as hell," Pat said.

"You could say that."

"Do you have any idea who killed her?" Lana asked.

"I guess her husband could have done it."

"When was the last time you saw your sister?" Pat asked.

"I never saw her after I left L.A. The next time I even heard about her is when I paid for the burial. I'm getting stuck with that, too."

"Isn't her husband helping with that?"

"Not if he can help it. His way is to let somebody else pay. Half the money he makes he gets from suckers who pay him to keep his mouth shut."

"Blackmail?"

"His profession, his hobby, and his love."

From his position at the door the proprietor was scowling in Millie's direction.

"I'd better go before he starts docking my pay," said Millie. "I've got nothing more to tell you, anyway."

Lana was reluctant to bring an interrogation to a close until she was sure she had gotten all there was to get. "What kind of life did she lead in Hollywood?" she asked.

"From what I've heard, she was a pretty naughty girl."

"What does that mean?" Lana asked.

"You figure it out," Millie said. She rose and left the table with her tail wagging sensuously.

At McCarran Airport they were early for their return flight. Pat wanted a drink and Lana didn't mind joining him. They both hated the thought of the bumpy ride ahead of them.

"This David Taylor is turning out to be quite a model citizen," Lana observed as she sipped her glass of chardonnay.

"Think he did it?" Pat asked. He drained his beer glass and poured the rest of the Coors into the glass.

"Why would he?" Lana asked. "Sounds like she was the breadwinner in the family."

"We don't have much to go on, do we?" Pat said.

"Not much. The investigating team interviewed everybody on the lot and came up with zilch."

"We do know the fire was set deliberately."

"Any guesses who set it?" Lana asked.

"Somebody who wanted to create enough confusion so he or she could sneak on the lot," Pat said.

"Would have been nice if there'd been fingerprints on the knife or if it could have been traced."

"No such luck."

"Guess we'd better head on home," Lana said.

"Not so fast," Pat said as he headed for the nearest slot machine. "I've got a couple of more quarters."

CHAPTER THIRTEEN

Going west on Pacific Coast Highway, Max Porter was still shouting into the car phone, oblivious to the bruised blue, pink and black of the sinking sun that was lighting the rim of the Pacific Ocean.

Oblivious also to the traffic that surrounded him, he came close to back-ending the blue BMW convertible ahead of him. He slammed on the brakes and screamed curses until he saw the muscular driver of the BMW open the door of the convertible. The man reached back into the car, removed a machete and walked with deliberation and clearly stated threat toward Max and his car.

Quickly Max slammed down the locks on the doors and windows, checked the traffic behind him, and with his middle finger raised in salute, floored the Mercedes and roared around the enraged driver. The driver ran several paces after Max's car, but Max was far down the road by that time. He cursed. It was becoming increasingly dangerous to get on the road in Los Angeles. If a driver didn't tailgate you, he could cut you off and cause you to have an accident no matter how good a driver you were. It was even worse on the freeways where drivers had to dodge junk dropped from overpasses or stray bullets that came from almost any direction. Max wondered what was making everybody so angry.

Max was already frustrated and angered when he pulled

through the sentry gate to the Colony. Driving into the driveway of the starkly modern beach house, he looked at it in distaste. It was all the real estate he had left after his first two marriages. He had hated the house from the beginning but had allowed the second wife to talk him into it. She had talked him into and out of a lot of things, including all of his cash, stocks and apartment buildings. "Bitch," he muttered as he walked toward the front door.

At least he felt better at the thought of the sexual activity that awaited him inside. One of the things that had surprised and delighted him when the relationship developed between him and the housekeeper was her willingness to indulge him at any time.

He removed his key ring from his pocket and inserted the key into the front door. The key turned in the lock, but when he pushed the door to open it, he realized that it was bolted from the inside. He also realized for the first time that the house was in total darkness.

"What the hell is going on here?" he said out loud.

He walked down the seldom-used, paved brick pathway that led to the ocean front. He stepped up on the deck and crossed to the French doors. This door, too, was bolted, but it was flimsier than the front door, and he kicked it repeatedly until the wood was splintered and the door sprung open.

His anger had now reached the point of rage, and it increased when there was no answer to his repeated calls for the housekeeper.

He decided that she had left him and that he was alone in the house. He crossed the living room and continued on past the library when he saw her there, in the half dark of dusk. She was sitting on the edge of the sofa, staring straight ahead with her jaw set in a forbidding way.

"What the fuck's going on?" he called.

She clicked on the television set with the automatic dial control she was holding in her hand. Curious, he crossed to the door in time to see the VCR light up. A tape had already been inserted.

"What show are you watching?" he asked, trying to decide what had come over her.

"Your show!" she said bitterly.

He recognized the two figures in the scene. It was a lovemaking scene and he remembered when it had been taken and wondered how the cameraman had taped it without his knowing. But then he remembered the frenzy of the intercourse and realized that a volcano could have erupted and he would have been unaware of it.

The girl was Lyla Taylor and the rear end pumping furiously up and down on her was his own.

He was unprepared for the fury of her fists when Elena threw herself against him. She scratched his face and pummeled his chest and tried to knee him in the groin until he wrapped his arms around her immobilizing her.

"Now what's all this about?" he demanded.

"You tell me you love me. You tell me you'll marry me, but you screw other women. I hate you."

"Where did you get this tape?"

"It came in the mail."

"Was it in a package?"

"Let go of me. I'll show you."

He released her, and she picked up a paper wrapping from the waste basket. Attached to it he found an envelope. In it was a note which said: "Enjoy! I'll be in touch." There was no signature, but it could only have come from David Taylor.

While he read the note, Elena's gaze had gone back to the tape still running in the VCR. The scene had switched now to a moment of seemingly genuine affection between Max, whose face was now clearly visible, and Lyla.

Elena burst into a new fit of anger and threw herself against

Max from behind, clenching him viselike in her arms and legs and biting him on the shoulder.

He shook her free, but she came at him again. This time she held an ashtray over her head, ready to throw it at him. He succeeded in grabbing the ashtray away from her and embraced her to prevent her assault on him. As he held her close, she squirmed in his arms, and he felt excitement rising in him. She felt it, too, and turned her body toward his. Together they fell onto the sofa. As they tore at each other's clothing, the tape, unnoticed, ran its course.

CHAPTER FOURTEEN

Lyla Taylor's body was being put to rest at Forest Lawn Cemetery.

The mourners were assembled on the terrace of the Wee Kirk O' The Heather Chapel in the Hollywood Hills. The grounds stretched for acres along Forest Lawn Drive and overlooked the Warner Bros. Studio where an action movie was being filmed. The ceremony was accompanied throughout by the sounds of gunfire and the director's voice shouting directions through his headset.

Pat O'Collins and Lana Slocum had arrived early and kept apart from the main group of friends and family. As unobtrusively as possible they observed the demeanor of the guests as they arrived.

A large number of them were acting students at the Gower Acting School which Lyla had attended. The proprietor, Antonia Barrett, was a former casting agent who had created the school when she was no longer employable as a network executive. She, too, was in attendance. She consoled her students, but at the same time pointed out that in life we are also in death and that they should live this moment. They could profit from the experience; if they ever had to act a role which called for bereavement, they could call it up.

Marty Miller had represented Lyla for only a short time, but he felt he would look bad unless he showed up. At the same time it would afford him an opportunity to meet young people with talent who might be looking for representation. One never knew when one might come upon the next Marlon Brando or Shirley MacLaine.

Emory Goode's arrival attracted the usual attention. He was escorting Ariel Smart. They lingered for a few moments before entering the chapel.

Emory had volunteered to be Ariel's escort, aware of Ariel's complicated feelings about Lyla's murder. She had confessed to him her ambivalence about the Tiffany role. On the one hand, she gloried in achieving it. On the other, she did not feel she had come by it honestly, and her satisfaction was lessened a great deal by guilt.

Emory tried to help her come to grips with the fact that she was qualified for the part, and that she deserved it.

"Who do you think killed Lyla?" she asked.

"I don't know, and the police don't seem to be getting anywhere."

"Maybe you ought to put that good mind of yours to work solving this case," Ariel said.

"I'm a director, not a detective."

"All the better. As a director you study what makes people do what they do. You know human nature. You understand motives. You always know how to get to the heart of a scene. You ought to be able to get to the heart of this problem."

"I'll put my mind to it," Emory said, half-joking, yet intrigued.

He was still mulling it over when Marty Miller came over and kissed Ariel on the cheek.

"I hear you're wonderful in the role, Ariel," he said.

"Thanks, Marty, but I've got a good director. It's all his doing."

"That's true," said Emory with a smile. "You ought to come to the studio and see your client work."

"I will, now that I know I'm welcome," he said and went on into the chapel.

★ ★ ★

"I think I've ruled her out," Lana said after studying Ariel for a moment.

"On what basis?" Pat asked.

"Innocent. She just doesn't look the type."

"Are you forgetting she got the part? We haven't checked out her alibi, and she was the one with the most to gain from this."

"I guess you're right, but I'm not so sure. She look like a killer to you?"

"Everybody in Hollywood looks like a killer to me, if they can gain something from it."

"You need to get out of town," Lana said. "You've gotten too cynical."

"That's what this job will do for you," he said. "Don't get me wrong. She's not my primary suspect, but we better check out her alibi."

"Who is your primary suspect?" she asked.

Before Pat could answer, his eye fell on the man who had just entered.

"I wonder what he's doing here," Pat said. Lana followed his look to Max Porter and a soberly dressed Elena Gomez who had walked up onto the terrace.

"He probably came to make sure all his cast and crew go right back to work as soon as possible."

"Tight, huh?"

"They say he's the worst. Is that his wife?" Lana asked.

"I don't know," Pat said. "You're the one who reads the tabloids."

"Last count he'd had two wives, but I don't think this is one of them."

All attention turned now to the procession arriving from the funeral home.

A hearse pulled up to the back of the chapel and four pall-bearers emerged to carry the body inside.

A limousine followed and two people got out. It was clear from their body language that they wanted to keep as much space between them as possible. The woman, Millie Flowers, in black dress and hat, bore a slight resemblance to the dead girl. The other person, David Taylor, dressed in a dark suit which looked as if it had been rented for the day, bore little resemblance to the bare-chested, bluejeaned man the two detectives had already interviewed.

"She looked better with her cat tail," Pat said.

"Don't joke," Lana said.

"Somebody cleaned up the husband pretty good and loaned him a suit."

"Looks deep in mourning to me," Lana said.

"He just looks spaced out to me," Pat said.

The front door of the chapel was opened gently and organ music wafted outside. A guest book had been set up on a pedestal by the entrance, but nobody had signed it.

On their way to the family seating area, David and his sister-in-law ignored each other, then sat as far as possible from each other.

"No love lost between those two," Lana observed from the rear of the chapel where she and Pat were watching the proceedings.

"Could he be the one who sliced her?" Pat asked.

"Why would he?" Lana asked.

"Well, she screwed half of Hollywood. He could have been jealous."

"Yes, but he made money out of that."

"She might have been holding out on him."

"What was he doing on the lot, and how did he get on?"

"He could have gotten on the lot like anybody else, because of the fire."

Antonia Barrett rose to deliver the eulogy.

"Lyla was one of those thousands of actors who arrive here every day. But unlike the majority, she had talent, determination, and beauty. And unlike the majority, she was about to get a break that would have put her over the top in our industry. Instead we are here to remember her. Because she was so professional I think she would want us not to mourn for her, but to dedicate ourselves to her memory by carrying on our own work."

Antonia continued her tribute to her late pupil, occasionally giving the girl such sterling qualities that no one among the mourners knew who she was talking about.

Suddenly a late-comer arrived at the back of the church. Silence fell while several faces turned toward the rear. Swiftly Justin Hargreaves found a seat beside the attractive woman sitting next to Max Porter. She gave him an enigmatic half smile and an appraising look.

Antonia kept on at length. It was a typical eulogy. No one would remember it by the time they reached grave side.

Emory was only half listening. His mind had flashed back to Ariel's suggestion that he might be able to solve the murder. He had, in fact, already been going over certain possibilities.

For instance, he thought, Marty Miller would make a possible suspect. Certainly he had a motive. He might have killed Lyla to make sure that his client, Ariel, got the job.

The husband was another suspect. Emory had read that family members were the most common killers, and from what he had read in the *Los Angeles Times* a husband could easily have reason to kill his wife in a jealous rage.

On the other hand, it could have been Ariel herself, but he dismissed that thought quickly since he had grown fond of her. He would much rather suspect Justin Hargreaves, who'd had every opportunity and had voiced his hatred for Lyla. But then, was Justin's dislike of her sufficient motivation to kill her? Sly rumors that he had picked up earlier about Max Porter's involvement with Lyla came to mind. Max was impulsive and emotional; perhaps Lyla did something that pushed him over the edge. With Max, anything was possible.

And the murderer could be someone they didn't know, someone not connected with show business at all, who might have had reason to kill Lyla.

And then the grim thought occurred to him: "There's me." The police had made a big deal out of the fact that he was the last person to see her alive. It would certainly be in his best interest to solve this murder, and soon.

There were considerably more mourners at graveside than usually followed from the chapel. Most of Lyla's classmates were there to absorb the experience for future use.

"Ashes to ashes, dust to dust," intoned the minister after the coffin had been lowered into the grave, and started to hand the shovel to David Taylor.

Millie Flowers stepped in front of her brother-in-law and took the shovel before he could grasp it.

"I don't think that's your place," she said.

"It's not yours, either," David said. The minister looked horrified.

"You might each participate," he said, trying to mollify them.

Now David reached for the shovel and a struggle ensued. The assembled group gasped in horror.

"You've got no right," Millie hissed. "You never really loved her. You abused her in every way. You're probably the one who killed her!"

From their position nearby the two detectives looked to each other meaningfully.

"How about them apples?" Pat said.

Lana said, "We know he's a bad boy, but would he kill his meal ticket?"

"This is Hollywood," said Pat, "where anything can happen."

"Let's get out of here," Lana said, and they walked back toward their car.

CHAPTER FIFTEEN

On the terrace of her penthouse, Roberta Goode bent over the miniature tree. It was a Japanese maple, part of her collection of bonsai, which she had collected and nurtured since before she was married.

The small trees meant a great deal to her. They could survive for hundreds of years if properly cared for. She loved their beauty and the fact that she was in control of their shape, their longevity and their health, in a world where she felt she had little control left.

She thought ruefully of the fact that the little maple was one she had planted the year Robin was born. It had been Robin's plant, and she had trained her daughter in the proper way to care for it. Now Robin was gone and the plant was healthy, while Robin most assuredly was not. Roberta's hands shook as she tended to the tree.

Caring for the plants in her penthouse garden was usually a solace and source of pleasure to her, but today her mind was in turmoil as she worried and wondered where Robin might be.

She was expecting the doorbell, and when it rang she left the terrace, crossed to the door and opened it to admit a portly white male detective and his partner, an attractive, somewhat slimmer black female.

"I've never been interrogated by detectives before," Roberta said. "Where do we begin?"

"This isn't exactly an interrogation," the Irish-looking one said. "We're trying to locate your daughter."

"So am I," Roberta said. "Why are you looking for Robin?"

"We have reason to believe she was acquainted with a young woman who was recently murdered, Lyla Taylor."

"The girl from *King's Harbor*?"

"Did you know her?" Lana said.

"She was in one of my husband's plays in New York. Why would my daughter be connected with her?"

"That's what we'd like to know. We found your daughter's name and address in the deceased woman's address book. We're checking on everybody who might have had a connection with her."

"I'm as mystified as you are," Roberta said.

"Do you have any idea where your daughter is?"

"I do not."

"Did you know that the murdered woman and her husband were drug dealers?"

"I wouldn't be surprised by that at all. From all I've heard, both of them were capable of a good many strange acts."

"Do you know any reason why the woman or her husband would have your daughter's name?"

Roberta thought for a moment, then, as much as it pained her, said, "My daughter is addicted to drugs. She seems to have fallen in with unsavory people."

"If we could talk to your daughter, we might be able to clean this matter up, at least remove her from the list of possible suspects."

Anger flared in Roberta's face.

"I've hardly had time to get used to my daughter's addiction, and now I learn she's suspected of murder. My daughter wouldn't kill anybody."

"We'll have to ask you to keep us informed if she comes home. We'll find her eventually, and I'm sure you'd like this settled as much as we would."

Lana Slocum extended her card, and when Roberta failed to take it, she left it on the table edge.

CHAPTER SIXTEEN

I t was a perfect night for the Golden Globe Awards, cool enough to dress up, but not so cold that those women who chose to display vast expanses of erotic flesh would be uncomfortable.

Over the years the Golden Globes had gained a status it had not enjoyed in the beginning. Started originally by a group of foreign journalists, only in recent years had it attracted top talent and big wheels in the industry.

Insiders had finally noticed that the Golden Globe winners were often indicators of who would later win the Emmys and the Oscars. And as more of the revenues from films and television came from foreign sources it cinched their importance. Top actors, directors, writers and executives felt obliged to attend, even though it sometimes meant being interviewed by an entertainment writer from some obscure third-world country.

The public cared little that the Golden Globes differed from any of the other award ceremonies. Huge numbers of fans were attracted to anything that brought out movie and television stars. Those in the industry gave awards endlessly to one another. Anything that would possibly increase the revenue of the series or the movie merited attention.

Fans had been gathering in front of the Pasadena Civic Auditorium for the past two days. Some had camped out in lawn chairs. Two of them had pitched tents until the Pasadena cops made them take them down. By the time the guests began arriving, every seat from the front row to the bleachers was packed with screaming, hollering, worshipping fans.

One young man with a crop of blond hair who walked with a mild limp strained to push his way through the crowd so that he might get closer to the arriving celebrities. He carried a placard which read: "Hi, Ariel." Nobody paid him any attention since few of them knew who Ariel was. He was just one of the many peculiar fans and curiosity seekers who thronged to such events. And the television cameras paid him no attention in favor of more famous faces.

Few recognizable faces arrived in the first wave. It was fashionable for the better-known stars to arrive as late as possible.

Pat O'Collins and Lana Slocum were two faces totally unknown to anybody. Lana, in her black, all-purpose formal, looked as enchanting as any actress, and an observer would have been hard pressed to guess that she was a detective. Pat would have had a hard time passing as anything more than what he was in his aged tuxedo. Together they circulated through the crowd on the lookout for suspicious behavior on the part of any of the suspects in the killing of Lyla Taylor.

On the periphery of the crowd, Marty Miller tried to get as close as possible to the arriving stars. He used every opportunity to impress possible clients and recruit new ones. An actor he had once represented drifted past and Marty reached out to shake his hand. The actor muttered "Prick" and brushed on past. Marty hoped no one had noticed.

An enormous roar swept across the bleachers when a long, white stretch limo arrived and a former champion boxer and his wife stepped out. Towering above his wife, the actor/pugilist man wore a gold lamé jacket over blue jeans, a black string tie and a blue chambray shirt. With a big, toothy smile, he waved to the crowd and then made his way to the interviewers who formed a gauntlet each celebrity had to run in order to enter the auditorium.

Mr. Blackwell, the self-styled arbiter of fashion, was commenting on a costume worn by a young starlet which he described as "something she could stuff back in her compact" when the show was over.

As the boxer arrived, Blackwell had no time to comment, as an interviewer ran after the actor and his wife.

Failing to catch the actor, the interviewer turned back to face Justin Hargreaves, who qualified for an interview as a well-known writer and one of this evening's nominees. Justin had received a nomination in the Best Script in an Original Drama category for his naturalistic depiction of small-town life in the Midwest today.

"Good luck tonight," said Deborah Savage, the interviewer, from *Paris Noir*.

"I don't think I stand much of a chance," Justin replied humbly.

"What are you working on now, Justin?" she asked.

"We've got a fabulous pilot in the works."

"I've heard good things about *King's Harbor*," Deborah replied.

"I'd like you to meet Ariel Smart who is playing the role of Tiffany in the pilot. Keep your eye on her. She's going to be a big star!"

"Well, we've got a wonderful script, and that's what makes a hit, you know," Ariel replied.

Ariel gave her best side to the camera and smiled appealingly. A look of wonder crossed her face when she caught sight of a sign that said "Hi, Ariel." She tried to see who might be waving the sign, but whoever it was was swallowed up in the undulation of the crowd.

"I've got a fan!" she exclaimed to Justin as they walked away from Deborah and farther down the red carpet into the auditorium.

"You'll have millions of them once you get on the air," he said.

Again the crowd roared its approval as Matthew Perry arrived, followed by Arnold Schwartzenegger and Maria Shriver.

Not as well-known but as spectacular was the arrival of Emory Goode and his companion for the evening. Emory defied traditional dress by wearing his usual costume of the vanilla ice cream suit and his white planter's hat. He stepped out of the limo and acknowledged the crowd's approval with a wave, then turned back and gave a hand to a stunning Native American actress as she stepped out of the limo.

Tawny Lost Eagle was more recognizable than he, since she had only recently starred in a modern version of the old Helen Hunt Jackson book *Ramona*. Valentino had designed her striking gown of blue silk embedded with turquoise stones that gave it a Navaho flavor.

She made her stately way through the crowd, stopping often to sign autographs and to touch majestically any outstretched hand.

"And here, ladies and gentlemen," said Deborah, "are two of this evening's most distinguished guests, director Emory Goode and Tawny Lost Eagle. Emory, as you know, is to receive a special award for directing 'Navaho Winter,' last year's historical drama which looks as if it's going to win every major award this year. With Emory is the star of 'Navaho Winter,' the gorgeous and talented Tawny Lost Eagle. Congratulations to both of you!"

"Thank you, Deborah," Emory said. With a courtly bow he brought her hand up to his lips and kissed it.

"Is he always this gallant?" Deborah asked Tawny.

"Not when he's working," Tawny said. "He's a demon when he puts on his director's hat."

The director and the actress swept on into the auditorium where an usher met them and conducted them to the private suite of rooms reserved for presenters and nominees.

★ ★ ★

"Who's that?" asked a fan in the crowd along the path from curb to entrance.

"Nobody," said the person next to him.

If Max Porter had heard the remark he would have told the speaker how wrong the speaker was and how rich he, Max, happened to be. But Max was preoccupied escorting the stunning woman he had rented for the evening. She was one of those women available in Hollywood for a price. Her price was higher than Max usually liked to spend, but it was fixed by the high price she usually received from visiting oil potentates.

"Smile," said Max.

"I am smiling," she said.

"That's what I'm paying you for," he said.

"Then are we skipping the rest of the evening?"

"No," replied Max, "at the price I'm paying we ought to be together for a week."

She smiled sweetly at him, and when someone held out an autograph book, she accepted it and signed the name of a well-known star.

The master of ceremonies was Jeff Roman, the tubby comedian who had made it from stand-up comedy to actor and finally to TV director. He had risen high partially because of a genuine talent for comedy, but even more important for his ability to kiss ass and a convenient marriage to an established comedienne. This evening was the most prestigious appearance so far in his career, and he struggled to keep his anxiety from showing. He was only somewhat successful.

His somersault entrance onto center stage unfortunately turned into a pratfall. The audience became confused and didn't realize he was trying to make a joke. Only a few uncertain giggles floated up from the audience.

"Good evening, Mr. and Mrs. America and all the ships at

sea!" he began, but nobody remembered that this had been Walter Winchell's standard opening, so they waited for a punch line that never arrived.

After his initial departure from the teleprompter, Roman went back to the prepared script. By then he had lost a good part of the audience, who sat numbly waiting for the celebrities to be paraded out like prize Herefords.

From her seat beside Justin Hargreaves Ariel Smart looked on with wonder. She could hardly believe that she was surrounded by some of the most illustrious names in show business. From where she sat she could almost reach out and touch Gina Lollabrigida, Goldie Hawn and Kurt Russell.

When the nominees for Best Original Script were being announced, Justin straightened up in his seat expectantly, took her hand and held it tightly.

His crossed fingers relaxed with disgust when the announcement was made and he found that John McGreevey had won in his place. Justin attempted a smile, but it became a sickly grin.

"Next year," she whispered.

"For both of us," he replied.

Midpoint in the evening the Orson Award was announced. It was no secret that Emory Goode was the recipient. The entire cast of *King's Harbor* rose in recognition, and the rest of the audience followed suit. The spotlight followed him from his seat to the podium.

The winner from the previous year, Valentine Larson, greeted him at the podium. They shook hands and Larson handed him the statuette.

Emory made a short, gracious acceptance speech and was escorted from the stage by a starlet to a room behind the stage where the press was waiting.

At the dance following the ceremony, Emory and his companion joined one of the tables reserved for *King's Harbor*. Justin Hargreaves was still in a bad mood and grieving for the lost award. Max Porter was barking at the waiter to bring another bottle of wine. He wanted to bring the evening to a close as quickly as possible, and his date became more and more alluring as each minute passed.

Ariel's agent, Marty Miller, stopped at the table. Max insulted him and he moved on to another table. He approached each new table with the same abject, obsequious air and mechanical smile.

"Congratulations, Ariel," said a voice behind her.

Every female at the table turned an appreciative eye to the blond surfer type who smiled down at Ariel.

Ariel rose and embraced the young man warmly.

"Everybody, this is my friend, Tim Dean."

Ariel called off the names of all those at the table.

Tim acknowledged each person, coming finally to Emory.

"Mr. Goode and I know each other," he said.

"Tim is a promising young actor," said Emory.

"I used to look like you when I was your age, Tim," said Max Porter facetiously. "You did some good work in that soap out of New York."

"I'm surprised you know that," Tim said.

"I make it my business to know those things."

Max turned to Emory. "Does this kid remind you of anyone?"

"Yes, I think he'd be perfect for the role of Derek."

"We ought to read him for that part tomorrow."

Justin noticed the smile that Ariel and Tim exchanged. The last thing he wanted was Ariel playing opposite a sexy young man.

Justin Hargreaves interrupted. "That part is for a brunette. And it's an important role. It's for a more experienced actor."

Max overrode the writer's objection.

"All the women will love him. He and Ariel will make a great team."

"Be at the studio tomorrow around three," Max said to the actor. "I'll have my secretary leave you a pass."

"Thank you, Mr. Porter," the young actor gave his most provocative smile to the table, but each of the women thought that the smile was for her alone.

"He's not right for the part," Justin said.

"I'll tell you who's right for the part," Max said.

At a table way in the back of the room known to the "in" crowd as *Siberia* sat Pat O'Collins and Lana Slocum. The other chairs at the table were empty.

"I guess you'd probably like to dance," Pat said.

"I've got two left feet," Lana replied.

"That's perfect. I've got two right feet."

"I remember from the last time at the Police Athletic League Dance," she said.

"Have you spotted anything worth mentioning?" Pat asked.

"Certainly not the entertainment," Lana replied.

"Emory Goode still your prime suspect?" Pat asked.

"He was the last one to see her alive," Lana said.

"But he had no motive that we know about."

"We found his daughter's name in Lyla's book. Maybe she's the one who turned his daughter on to dope."

"But did he know that?"

"We can't be sure, but if it were true he'd have one honey of a motive."

"Actually Justin Hargreaves had the clearest motive to do the girl in. He wanted to cast the girl sitting right next to him now. He was on the lot that night, and they say he's got a trigger temper."

"Yes, but would he kill over a casting disagreement?"

"We'd better check his background."

"And Ariel Smart claims she was out of town. I checked the hotel where she claimed she stayed and they had her registered."

"And there's always the old X factor. Somebody we haven't

even come across yet."

They shared a companionable smile and each of them had another glass of wine.

Much of the crowd still lingered. Fans were unwilling to go home until the last autograph had been collected and they'd had the last glimpse of their idols.

Couples straggled out to wait in line for their limos to pick them up. As a client headed for the pick-up station, the driver, notified by walkie-talkie, left the parking lot and arrived at about the same time as his client.

Max Porter and his companion for the evening were chatting with another couple on their way to the car. Max stopped and was shaking hands with the other man when suddenly a woman burst through the crowd across the red velvet rope and called out, "You son of a bitch!"

The moment came so abruptly that afterwards, looking back, it seemed to be in slow motion.

The woman was Elena and she held a butcher knife high over her head. When it was only inches from his back, Max's companion raised her purse and deflected the knife. There were screams and gasps as some people fled, but the man Max had been talking to had the presence of mind to grasp Elena's arm and wrestle her to the ground.

The confusion attracted Pat O'Collins and Lana Slocum, and when they saw Elena and the man who held her, they hurried to them.

Elena was still spitting and hurling curses at Max Porter as the police hauled her away.

CHAPTER SEVENTEEN

Ariel was asleep when the phone rang. When she picked up the receiver and heard Tim Dean's voice, she wasn't the least bit annoyed.

"I've got that audition today," he explained, "and with that kind of ammunition I might get an agent to take me on."

"I'm sure you can," Ariel said.

"I know a lot of agents from the restaurant, but they're mostly big time and wouldn't take me on. I was wondering about your guy. What do you think of Marty Miller?"

"He works hard. And he did get me this job."

"I'm going to try him," Tim said.

"Good luck," she said.

Armed with the phone number and address Ariel had given him, Tim set out for the agent's office. He was surprised to find that it was in a run-down office building in Culver City.

Miller obviously had not expected a caller at such an early hour. When he came to the door, Tim noticed in the room beyond a fold-away cot and the aroma of boiling coffee and burnt toast.

"Be with you in a minute," Marty said after Tim explained why he was there.

The wait was longer than a minute, and by the time Tim was admitted to the office the rollaway bed, the coffee pot and the toaster had been stowed away and the room resembled a modest business office.

Tim was having misgivings about an agent who seemed to live in his office, and his apprehension showed in his face. Marty took pains immediately to remedy the situation.

"Sometimes I spend the night here," Marty lied, who spent every night there. "When I get busy I just stay over. My clients' lives are more important to me than my own."

He looked at Tim to see how his story was going over with the young actor. Tim's face revealed little.

"So Ariel recommended me," Marty said. "I've made some wonderful deals for her, and now she's on her way to the top."

He leaned back in his chair, made a tent with the tips of his fingers and used it to support his chin.

"Now, what can I do for you, Tim?"

"I have an audition this afternoon, and I want some kind of representation before I go in."

"Smart boy," Marty exclaimed. "What's the role?"

"Part of Derek on *King's Harbor.*"

"I know that role. It's a good showcase for an actor. I know just the kind of deal to make for you, and I should tell you that I'm very close to Max Porter."

"Can't hurt," Tim said, feeling a small surge of confidence.

"Here are the agency papers," Marty said and handed over a pen. "You'll need to sign in all the places indicated. I'll fill in the blanks later."

"I'll take them along and look them over," Tim said.

"I can only represent you this afternoon if we have signed papers," Marty said.

"I'll take my chances and get back to you."

The agent was less than satisfied. Other potential clients had checked up on his reputation and subsequently refused to sign with him.

★   ★   ★

Max Porter woke in a house that was unusually quiet. He had become accustomed to waking with Elena's warm body nestled against his. She would waken and make coffee and bring it to him when he was only half-awake.

For a moment he reached to where her body should be, and when it was not, events of last night came to him with a powerful rush. He was afraid to turn on the television set or check the newspapers. He was certain his picture and a story would be there, and he was right. He was thankful that Gloria, his paid companion, had split and happily was not in the newspaper story.

He looked at his picture in the newspaper and saw the fear in his eyes. But this morning he felt not fear but anguish over the way he was pictured. His hair was tousled, his tux had been dis-arranged, and Elena was clearly spitting in his face as she was being hauled away.

"Damn bitch," he muttered.

He got up and made his own coffee. It took him some time to find all the necessary components and by the time the coffee was ready he had decided he must go and get her. He wanted to keep her from giving out too much information about him, and at the same time he knew he needed her. Besides, the coffee was bitter.

Before he left for the jail he called his office and demanded a call-back in his car with a "flash report" on the financial status of his production company as well as the overnight ratings of all of his shows.

"And make it snappy!" he snarled. Backing out of the garage he nearly ran over a jogger.

"Fuck you," he called, raised his index finger and sped away.

While Max was obtaining her release, Elena was smart enough to remain compliant so long as they were in the Pasadena Police Station. But as soon as they reached the sidewalk, she turned on him and declared, "I am not going home with you."

"Where in the hell will you go then? You're a wetback without a green card, you got no money, no trade."

"I am not a wetback. I don't need a green card. What I want is to be treated like a real woman. I'm twice as pretty as that bitch whore you had hanging off your arm last night. I take the best care of you, and you treat me like a scrubwoman!"

"Get in the car. We'll talk in the car."

"We'll talk right here."

Max turned and walked toward the driver's side of the car.

"Make up your mind," he called over to her. "I'm leaving."

"Fuck you," she said.

Max started the engine of the Mercedes and pulled away from the curb.

Elena ran after him, and when he slowed she began beating on the windshield.

"I'll kill you," she screamed. "I will break in your house and cut your throat. You are a mean son-of-a-bitch, and I am out of your bed for good!"

The two policemen coming out of the station stopped and smiled at each other. They had just seen Max release Elena and had predicted just this kind of scene once she was out of the station.

What they had not predicted was that after her tirade, Elena opened the rear door of the Mercedes, climbed in, and was still shouting threats at Max as the car sped away.

CHAPTER EIGHTEEN

S herwin Fields was shrewd enough to know that power depended not only upon his relationship with Gerald Walker, but also on his relationships with the suppliers of the shows on the networks. It was his practice to let the suppliers know that he had the power, and that when they needed something they had to come to him.

From time to time, he made surprise visits to the sets of the various programs while they were in production. Often he left in his wake fear, anger, frustration and hatred to say nothing of subverted program content. In one famous case the program itself never recovered and was canceled.

The first thing Sherwin requested when he surprised the cast and crew on Stage 23 was an immediate change of costume on Tiffany King, the role played by Ariel Smart.

"I want a little more cleavage," he said to the wardrobe mistress. "And I want the dress shorter and tighter."

"She's supposed to be a girl with class, not a whore," objected the wardrobe mistress.

"Nobody likes nice girls," he responded.

The wardrobe mistress went back to her trailer and called the production office. The only person there was Justin Hargreaves, working as usual on the script.

"There's a man here from the network, and he's making all kinds of suggestions for changes."

"What man?" Justin asked.

"He says he's Gerald Walker's right-hand man. I think somebody from up there had better get down here. I don't know how to deal with him."

"What does he want?" Justin asked.

"It sounds to me like he's trying to turn Tiffany into a hooker."

"Good God," Justin said. "Don't do a thing. I'll be right down."

Justin was boiling with indignation by the time he reached Stage 23, his ears and the tip of his nose flaming red. He found Sherwin Fields rearranging the furniture in the main salon of the yacht. Fields had already replaced the draperies, and the prop people were frantically showing him new pieces of furniture for his approval.

When he spotted the writer coming toward him, visibly upset, Sherwin looked up with a smile.

"Hello, Justin, I'm so glad you're here."

"What's going on here?"

"Gerald has been so unhappy that he asked me to come out and take care of some of his concerns."

"Tiffany is not a slut!" Justin could not keep the anger and indignation out of his voice.

"Nobody says she is," Sherwin said. "What we've got to do is make her more beautiful and more appealing to the audience. The actress has a good figure. Why waste it?"

"The costume has to help define the character," Justin said.

"That's what I'm trying to do."

"Like hell you are. From now on if you want changes made, make them through our office and not directly to department heads."

"I would have, but there were no executives on the set," Sherwin said with his usual sly smile. He seemed to imply that things would go to hell unless he checked up all the time.

"Then you shouldn't have come at the crack of dawn. And what the hell is going on on the yacht set?"

"I made a few suggestions about the furnishings. They look dowdy, not opulent enough. You know how Gerald insists on a high tone to his sets."

"I was making a story point with the way the furniture looked. The King family is supposed to need money at the moment. They can't afford to refurnish."

"So in the meantime, the audience has to look at a cheap looking set that will make them switch channels?"

"If all they tune in for is to look at the set, I don't want them in my audience," Justin said and knew immediately that he had hanged himself.

"I won't mention to Gerald that you said that," Sherwin said in a very quiet voice. "Now let's move to the script. I've got just a few notes here. Won't take any time at all."

"What do you mean, notes? This script has been approved already. We're shooting the goddamned thing!"

He had heard horror stories about network interference but had never been part of it himself.

Justin tried to tell himself it was just a script, it was just a television pilot, but he had put too much of himself into the project, had spent too many late night hours working on the script. In truth, he honestly cared for the project and now, when he saw it threatened and quite possibly killed, he could not restrain his anger.

"Not big notes," Sherwin said. "Just some refinements that Gerald would like made. When you hear them, I'm sure you'll agree."

"I'm listening." Justin was apprehensive. He knew from past experience that Sherwin would make notes just to make notes and had little understanding of what made a dramatic script work.

"We feel that Derek's character is a little too puritanical. As written, he's practically angelic. We want a flesh and blood person, sort of an animal like Marlon Brando was in 'Streetcar.' We want a passionate relationship between Tiffany and Derek that the women in the audience will go crazy for. You do remember the audience, don't you, Justin?"

"I've got that relationship in the script, but you have to work up to it," Justin said defensively. "They can't just say hello and jump straight into bed. We've got to feel that they want to make love even before they do it."

By this time Justin's mouth was dry and he could barely croak. "We've got to get Max into this conversation," he said.

"Shall we go up to his office?" Sherwin asked.

Justin said. "He's not in yet."

"Then what do you suggest we do?"

"We're going to have to shut down if we do half the things you're talking about," Justin replied resentfully.

Emory Goode approached in time to hear the words "shut down," and he was not pleased. Nor was he happy to see that the salon of the yacht was not ready for shooting.

"Will someone kindly tell me why my set is not ready?" he asked politely.

The crew had been lurking in the background but listening intently to every word.

"Gerald wanted a few changes," Sherwin said.

"You tell Gerald if he wants a few changes he can speak to me. I want that set put back just the way I had it yesterday. Now let's get to work."

"You can't do this, Emory," Sherwin said.

"Watch me," said Emory. "Nobody will touch anything. Unless it's done my way, I'm pulling the plug on the show."

"Fellows," Emory said to the crew, "do what I told you and let's get to work. We've got a show to shoot."

Emory turned to Sherwin, whose face had gone white with disbelief. "I want you off this set. If you're not gone in one minute, I'm going to kick your ass out of here."

"I won't forget this, Emory," Sherwin said.

"I hope not," Emory said. He turned back to the set and called, "Places everybody! Let's have a rehearsal."

At the sound recording studio on Burbank Boulevard, the receptionist observed the young girl with some distrust. She was thin, and her eyes betrayed a lack of sleep and a certain desperation.

"I've got to see my brother," Robin said.

"What's your brother's name?"

"David Taylor. He's the clarinetist."

"They're recording right now. Why don't you wait around? They'll be taking a break in about ten minutes."

Robin sat for a moment, then got up and went to the ladies' room. When she came out she paced rapidly up and down the reception area. After a while she became conscious that her erratic behavior was attracting the attention of the receptionist.

She took her seat again and clenched her hands together, trying hard to control the turmoil seething inside of her.

The red light over the door to the recording studio changed to green, and the musicians streamed out.

Robin rose and stood waiting at the door. When David Taylor emerged, already lighting his cigarette, he looked at her resentfully. He started to walk on past her when she plucked convulsively at the sleeve of his shirt.

"I've got to see you," she pleaded.

"Get lost," he said, looking around, hoping nobody had noticed.

"I'm going to scream," she threatened in a hoarse whisper.

"I haven't got any stuff on me," he said, trying to keep his voice low.

"I'm dying," she said. "You've got to help me."

He brushed past her and walked through the group of musicians who were looking at him with open curiosity.

In the parking lot he walked a short distance from the studio. The girl followed.

"Are you crazy?" he demanded. She continued to pluck at him as if somehow to draw from him what she needed.

"I'll do anything," she said.

"Just go away," he said.

"You're my only hope," said Robin.

"I don't carry shit on me," he said harshly.

"If Lyla were here, she'd help me."

"Lyla's dead," David said. "And don't blame her for your habit."

"Oh, but I do." Robin said. "I'd never even touched dope until she turned me on to it."

"No way," David said.

"Uh huh," Robin replied. "She was in a play in New York my father was directing and one day backstage she gave me my first hit. After that I was hooked."

"Does your old man know that?" David asked.

"I certainly never told him," Robin said. "Listen, I'm desperate. If you don't take care of me I'm going to scream."

"I've got to be careful. I think they're watching me. And I sure as hell am not going to deal here on the job."

"I could meet you some other place," Robin pleaded.

He threw down the butt of his cigarette and ground it out savagely with his heel.

"Shape up your life, kid," he said. "Go home to your folks!"

He turned and entered the building. Robin stood lost and alone, then wandered aimlessly away.

CHAPTER NINETEEN

The audition for the role of Derek, Ariel's love interest in *King's Harbor,* was being held in Max Porter's office, an indication of the importance of the role. Max did not ordinarily participate in casting, preferring to approve or disapprove a selection after the candidates had been weeded down to only a few.

The actor, Tim Dean, had learned his way around such casting sessions and was smart enough to aim his performance straight to Max Porter, who he knew would make the final decision.

As he and Ariel read the test scene it became obvious that there was chemistry between them and that the relationship would be beneficial to the series.

Ariel helped by giving Tim every opportunity to dominate the scene, to use it to show off his talent.

When they reached the end of the scene Max said, "You kids leave the room and we'll talk about you behind your backs."

At the door the young actor turned back, smiled, and said, "Thank you."

"Don't leave town, Tim," Max said as Tim and Ariel closed the door behind themselves.

"That's our boy!" Max exclaimed.

"The only thing that concerns me," Emory said, "is his lack of experience, but I can take care of that."

"Means we can get him cheap," Max said.

"I'm not interested in cheap," Emory said. "I want a show that's up to my usual standards and will be a credit to your company."

"Okay," Max said, "But you'd also better get interested in the money. I went over the budget this morning and the cost of this show is beginning to scare me."

Max turned to the business affairs executive, who seemed to be a bundle of jangled nerves.

"Get in touch with his agent and make a deal," said Max. "I don't want to spend any money on this kid. Who represents him?"

"He hasn't signed with anybody yet, but it looks like it's going to be Marty Miller."

"Good," Max said.

"Now everybody hold on a second," said an aggrieved voice. It was Justin Hargreaves who until now had remained silently disapproving.

"The actor's wrong for the part."

A silence fell in the room. It was not customary to publicly object to a decision once Max had reached one. Justin was aware of that unwritten rule, but his feeling were too strong to suppress.

"What makes you the expert?" Max demanded in an ice-cold voice.

"I created this pilot. I created this role. I created Derek especially to give Ariel a love interest. He's all wrong. He's got no depth."

"He's got balls," Max said. "That's what the women in the audience care about. I'm going to do a publicity push on him. Build up an off-stage romance between him and Ariel."

"I don't think you've got to do much invention," Emory said. "Looks to me like there's something going on there already."

"What are you looking so down in the mouth about?" Max

demanded of the writer.

"The actor is wrong for the role."

"I think I know what's wrong here. You're hot for the broad yourself."

"She's not a broad."

"If I say she's a broad, she's a broad. She's probably in the sack with that actor by now."

"At last we've got our actor," Emory said. "He and Ariel are going to make a wonderful pair."

"And, Justin, you'll feel better when you see the ratings skyrocket."

"Justin will feel better when he gets his paycheck," Max said. "This meeting's over. Let get on with the show."

★ ★ ★

CURTIS HUGHES' JOURNAL

God works in mysterious ways. They fired me at Hell for not showing up for work the night of the Globes, but the very next day I got on as a busboy at the Studio commissary. Not much money, but I can keep an eye on Ariel in the daytime now as well as at night.

I found out she doesn't come to the dining room every day. Somebody takes her lunch to her dressing room. I'll do my best to get that job.

There's a lot of talk around the studio about how good she is in the role. It doesn't surprise me, and I'm glad I helped make it happen.

The new guy is okay, and there is talk something might be going on. I'm sure that's not true. He just isn't on the same level as she is. She's got better taste than that. She'll know when her real love makes himself known.

★ ★ ★

"Cheers," Ariel said after the waiter poured the Perrier Jouet.

"I've got a job," Tim said in wonder. He looked around the bar crowded with attractive young Manhattan Beach people, a tanned, sleek crowd of young people on their way up in their professions.

"I owe it all to you," Tim said.

"You don't, but I'm glad you feel that way," Ariel said. "Now shut up and drink your champagne."

They touched their glasses together. Ruefully, Tim said, "On my first paycheck I'll buy you champagne."

"That's a date," she said.

"Here's to us," he said. "I've been wishing this could happen for a long time."

"Me too."

When the waiter arrived they ordered another bottle of champagne which they took with them out onto the beach.

In silence they looked out across the silver-tipped waves as they rolled in, lapping at the sand at their feet.

He kissed her, and as their bodies came close each knew what was in store for them. Arm in arm they walked toward her apartment.

The curtains were drawn and the room was in semi-darkness. Beyond the window the sound of the surf rose and fell in rhythmic undulation that matched the movement of the two bodies on the bed.

They moved together in response to their mutual need, each thinking only of the other. Tim paced himself until he could feel Ariel's climb toward that special moment.

And then he could no longer hold back, nor could she, and together they reached shared ecstasy. They held each other close while their passion subsided in diminishing waves.

He smiled at her, and she nestled closer as a blanket of contentment settled over them. They closed their eyes after a while and slept in each other's arms.

CHAPTER TWENTY

"Why don't you wait here, and I'll check out the building behind us," Emory said.

"Are you sure?" Roberta asked. "That building looks as if it might cave in any minute."

"Worth a look," he said. "It's exactly the kind of place these kids hole up in."

There had been a plywood board over the front door at one time, but it had been torn away and, now covered with graffiti, lay flat on the street in front of the building.

Emory entered the vile-smelling hallway. Odors of rat excrement and human urine assailed his nostrils. He wanted to turn back, but he made himself push on up the stairway.

From somewhere above streamed a pale light and the sporadic sound of voices.

He continued up the rickety stairway until he came to the landing. Now he could see the light streaming from underneath a closed door.

He crossed to the door and opened it. The smell of marijuana was intense, and a cloud of smoke hung over the room. The light came from an oversized candle in the middle of the room. Around it were several teenagers. Even in the dim light, Emory could tell that most of them had spiked hair of various startling colors and rings hanging from many unnatural parts of their faces.

"Your kid ain't here," called a male voice.

"Her name's Robin. Could you help, please?"

"What's it worth to you?"

Emory produced two twenty-dollar bills and held them out to the young man in front of him. He had purple hair and a tattooed tear drop beneath one eye. He accepted the money Emory held out towards him.

"You're Robin's daddy," he said sarcastically.

"I am, and I'm very worried," said Emory.

"Little late now," said Purple Hair.

"Have you any idea where I might find her?"

"We move around. She's young. The cops pick up the young ones. Try the Hollywood Division."

"I already have."

"Well, if she turns up, we'll pass it along that you're looking for her."

"Her mother and I would appreciate that."

"No luck?" Roberta asked when he emerged from the crumbling building.

"According to her friends, it's too late."

"That's what worries me," Roberta said. "Any more ideas?"

"Let's try that building across the street," Emory said and they trudged wearily in that direction.

Max Porter was shouting into the phone when Justin entered the office. The producer waved the writer to a seat and kept scolding the company accountant on the other end of the line for not holding back checks until the last possible moment. It was a standard practice so that the company could accumulate additional interest on the held-back money.

"What do you want?" Max barked as he hung up the phone.

"You wanted to see me?"

"You're damned right I want to see you. I just got those

revised pages! You're fucking up the script! I know why, and you're not going to get away with it!"

"I have no idea what you're talking about," Justin said innocently, avoiding Max's eye.

"Don't pull that innocent shit on me," Max said. "I was getting away with stuff like that when I was twelve years old."

"Explain 'stuff like that'."

"Stuff like writing dialogue that you know will trip Tim up and make him look bad."

"Why would I do a silly thing like that?"

"Come on, Justin, don't play dumb with me. Everybody knows you've got the hots for Ariel Smart and you're jealous of that kid with the big dick. He's getting it every night and you're home jerking off."

"What if I say you're right? I do like Ariel, but mainly I know what's best for the show."

"I know what's best for the show, and if you keep this shit up I'm going to hire another writer."

There was silence from the writer. He knew the threat was real, and he did not want to risk any further discussion.

"Go back to your office and fix this script," Max said, throwing the script into Justin's lap.

Emory stopped shooting and dismissed the cast and crew at four in the afternoon. Immediately, he received an irate call from Max Porter.

"What in the hell are you closing down for?" Max screamed. "You're throwing away two good hours of filming time."

"I'm giving my actors and my crew time to go home and get ready for that expensive party you're throwing tonight."

"That's another thing. When we go to series you've got to give me a couple of cheap episodes so I can make back what I'm spending on that party tonight."

"But, Max, the network's paying for this party, not you."

"Don't you ever close down the set early without asking me first," Max said trying to change the subject.

"I'll call the shots on the set. You've put me in charge here, and I'm going to be in charge. If you don't like that, you can get yourself another director."

Each man slammed down the phone at the same time.

CHAPTER TWENTY-ONE

I
t was customary for the network to give a get-acquaint-
ed party for each new pilot if it looked promising. Having seen a few of the dailies, the network decided that
King's Harbor looked decidedly promising and had
engaged the private party room upstairs at the Beverly Hilton
Hotel.

The blasé valets at the front entrance recognized that this
was a party for a television series pilot as soon as the guests started arriving in modest automobiles. They were mere members of
the crew. The stars and top executives would be arriving in rented limousines.

Marty Miller was among the first guests to arrive. He had
parked his car two blocks away to avoid paying for parking and
the valet tip. Once at the front entrance, he lurked at the periphery of the crowd, rushing over to pay obsequious homage to anyone who was half recognizable from their work in film.

The private party room had been decorated earlier in the day
with a nautical theme similar to the luxury yacht reproduced on
the set.

The bar was already crowded with drivers, grips, caterers and
their wives who knew everything that went on on the set and
were more privy to gossip than most of the actors. Among the
less renowned crew were Justin Hargreaves and Molly Thurston,
the casting director.

"I'm planning on getting very drunk tonight," Justin said.

"You're already well on your way," Molly observed. "Just don't plan on taking me home."

"I hadn't," he said.

"You are such a bastard," she said. "No wonder your women all leave you."

"You're beautiful when you're ornery," he said. "And my women leave me because I strike them regularly."

"I recognize the dialogue from the *King's Harbor* script. Who wrote it for you?"

"Shut up and drink," the writer said and signaled to the barman.

"I do vow and declare," Justin said as his gaze went to the entrance where Max Porter was making an unusually quiet entrance. With him was an exotic, dark-haired woman dressed in an Indian sari. She moved with a certain feline grace, but her carriage suggested an inner lack of confidence as if she had no right to be here.

"Who is she?" Justin asked. "Where have I seen her before?"

"Beats me," Molly said. "She's way out in front of most of those broads he turns up with."

"She looks like she came out of a cake at a stag party," Justin said.

"Actually, she works for Max," said a voice beside him. He turned to see Emory Goode, who was escorting an attractive, short-haired brunette woman in a tailored suit.

"Say hello to my wife, Roberta."

Pleasantries were exchanged and more drinks ordered.

Molly asked, "What does she do for Max?"

"If I'm not mistaken, one thing she does for him is embarrass him in public places," Emory said. "I'd almost swear she's the one who went for him at the Golden Globes."

"I recognize her now from the picture," Justin said.

"I suppose we ought to join them," Emory said and led the

way across the room to their table.

"I need a drink," Elena was saying.

"You had three in the kitchen before we left home," Max reminded her.

"I was nervous," she said, looking around the room in a guarded way.

"You're going to get drunk if you keep this up. Slow down."

"You are ashamed of me," she said. "You have not introduced me to your friends."

"These aren't friends. Just people who work for me."

"Can we join you?" Emory asked, as he and his wife and Justin and Molly approached the table. After introductions were made, Elena looked around the table and asked, "Will somebody please get me a drink?"

"I will," Justin volunteered.

"No, you won't," Max said. "She's had too much already."

Sullenly,, Elena began unwrapping the sari from around her shoulders.

"Keep your clothes on," Max ordered.

"It's warm in here," she said. "And it scratches."

"You just like showing your tits," he observed.

"You never mind looking."

The others in the group looked away in embarrassment.

"I thought you two were divorced," Max said to Emory and Roberta, trying to change the subject.

"We're separated," Roberta said. "But we're still friends."

"I'm still friends with all my ex-wives," Max said.

"How come you didn't invite them tonight?" Justin asked sarcastically.

"How are you doing with that script I told you to fix?"

"First thing in the morning."

"Writers never want to work," Max announced to the table. "Jack Warner was right. They're all schmucks with typewriters."

★ ★ ★

The paparazzi had gathered earlier on a tip that George Clooney was dining in the hotel, a report that turned out to be erroneous. But finding a function about to get underway, they stayed and took their chances that someone memorable might show up.

"Who's the beautiful girl?" asked the correspondent from the Valley News when Ariel and Tim arrived.

"That's my client," Marty said. "Her name's Ariel Smart, and she's taking over the star role in this new pilot. Spielberg's already after her to do a movie when she goes on hiatus."

"The boy with her anybody?"

"Not yet, but I've just signed him, and I'll soon have him on his way."

Within moments Ariel and Tim were surrounded by popping flash bulbs and photographers shoving each other for position.

Marty Miller inched his way to Ariel's side and whispered, "Hello, gorgeous."

She looked down at him for a moment as if she wondered who he was and where she might have met him.

"I'm your agent," he announced.

"Oh," she said, " . . . in all the excitement and all, I didn't recognize you." And then she turned to give the photographers one more magnetic smile.

"I mentioned you at DreamWorks today," chirped Marty, but she didn't hear him over the din of photographers voices. She entered the hotel on Tim's arm. Marty Miller followed, his head disappearing immediately among the taller guests.

At the entrance to the ballroom, a reporter from Variety stepped up to Ariel and introduced himself. He handed her a copy of his column for tomorrow's Variety.

Dazzling new star sails into King's Harbor *pilot,* blazed the headline. Ariel looked blankly at her date. "He's talking about you!" Tim said.

Ariel paused in the doorway for just the right amount of time, letting every eye come to rest on her in the time-honored way stars made their entrances. Only then did she start into the room. Simultaneously, the applause began and it built to a sweet and gratifying roar as her colleagues recognized the entrance of a brand new star.

"Kind of chokes you up, doesn't it," Justin said.

"I think it's rather nice," Roberta said. "Emory tells me she's a fine actress."

"Don't tell her that," Max said. "She'll want a raise."

Wine had been delivered to the table, and Elena was already gazing into her empty glass.

When she reached for the wine bottle, Max restrained her. "You've had enough," he said.

"Take your hand away from me," she said. When he did, she filled her wine glass to the brim. The sari had fallen completely away revealing an appealing expanse of bosom.

Ariel and her escort made their way through the admiring crowd. Her agent trailed along behind as if to share in his client's glory. She stopped frequently to accept congratulations. When they came to Max's table everyone except Elena rose in recognition.

"Get chairs for everybody, Marty," Max said to the agent who obediently began moving chairs from the adjacent table.

"I want to dance," Elena announced.

"There's no music," Max said.

"Tell the orchestra," she said.

"Get a hold of yourself," he advised her.

"Army Archerd gave Ariel a terrific mention," Marty said.

"I knew she was good when I hired her," Max said. "I don't need Army to tell me I've got a winner."

"You and I need to talk," Marty said. "I . . ."

"I'm a very busy man, Marty. Call my office and we'll see if we can work you in in the next couple of weeks."

At the first strains of the orchestra playing the theme song for *King's Harbor*, Elena, unnoticed for a moment, rose and started away from the table, undulating her hips in an enthusiastic belly dance.

Max looked after her impatiently.

"What does that broad think she's doing now?"

"I think she's had a little too much to drink," Ariel said.

Elena took a position and managed to gyrate her hips in a way that seemed to defy the limits of human anatomy. The orchestra leader took his cue from her dance and began an accompaniment, which increased her fervor. A crowd began to gather and clap rhythmically to each of her sensual movements which increased in speed and suggestion with each rolling wave of her hips.

"Maybe you ought to go over and rescue her," Roberta said to Max.

"Get her out of here," Max said to Justin.

"She's not my date," he objected.

"Get her out of here," Max repeated.

"No," Justin said.

"I'll handle it for you, Max." Everyone looked to Marty, who had been lurking at the edge of the group.

"No, I want Justin to do it," Max said firmly. "He's got to leave early to finish his script anyway."

Knowing he was defeated, Justin rose and shrugged to the casting director. "I'm sorry," he said, and crossed to Elena.

"We'll take Molly home," Roberta offered.

By now the dance and the music had built to a sensual frenzy. Other dancers had joined in and several had begun shedding garments.

Justin could see that Elena was beyond reason, so he joined in the dance and offered himself as her partner. She had abandoned all restraint. Her freedom of movement, the music and the moment worked its magic also upon Justin, and he found to his amazement that all of his inhibitions were slipping away. Together they performed a dance that was sexual, vigorous and liberated. The other dancers fell back and looked on, clapping in time to the music and the dance. Justin was hypnotized. He wanted her, and he wanted her alone. While he danced he began to back away. She followed and when they reached the exit they continued dancing until they were out of sight.

At Max's beach house, Justin supported Elena to the door.

"Can you make it from here?" he asked.

She fumbled with the key.

"No," she said. "You'd better help me inside."

He helped her all the way to her bed.

"Don't leave me now," she said.

CHAPTER TWENTY-TWO

Max Porter's office had been designed to magnify him physically. The furniture was arranged so that depending upon where he sat, the visitor could either be intimidated or made comfortable. Intimidation was accomplished by the lighting over the imposing chair behind the marble desk. If comfort and intimacy were the object, Max came from behind the desk, stepped down into the arrangement of chairs and sofas to the same level as the visitor.

Out of deference to *King's Harbor*, an original Winslow Homer seascape hung above the fireplace. Beyond the expanse of glass, the Hollywood sign was clearly visible, and, on past it, the outline of snow-capped mountains.

When Max realized that Ariel Smart, in her inexperience, was about to blurt out the reason for her visit, he directed her attention to the painting.

"I've always loved Homer," he said. He had never heard of Winslow Homer until the decorator brought in the painting and pointed out that it could be deducted from his income tax as a business expense.

"I'd never even seen the ocean until I came out here," Ariel said. She tried to find the words she had prepared to use with him, but somehow she had been thrown off course, and Max was now directing the conversation.

"You'll be able to buy your own yacht now that you're one of us," Max said.

"I'm glad you brought that up," she said. "I'm not getting paid enough money for my work."

Max looked shocked.

"One thing we ought to get straight. I'm your friend and your producer. We don't talk money. You've got an agent now to handle that for you."

"Have you seen my contract?" she asked.

Of course he had seen her contract. He had dictated every word of it and was well aware of the raw deal she had been handed.

"I don't get into those details. My business affairs people handle matters like that."

"Well, that may be, but everybody tells me that if this pilot sells, it will mean millions to your company and that, as the star, I should get a fair share of some of that money."

Her voice began to tremble. She felt as if she were defying her father and he was most displeased with her.

"I just thought you ought to know how I feel," she said.

"Let me look over your contract when it comes across my desk," Max said.

"Oh, come on, Max. You know darn well what my deal is, and you know it isn't enough."

"Honey, this is a conversation you should be having with your agent."

"I've had this conversation with my agent. He says there's nothing that can be done. I have to live with it, at least for the coming year. But I don't think it's fair."

She sat back down and waited. He moved closer to her and spoke in a fatherly fashion.

"What do you really think of your agent?"

"Not much."

"How long have you signed with him for?"

"Well, the agency contract is for two years, but I haven't signed it yet."

"Smart girl."

"That's my name."

"Then live up to it and dump him," Max said.

"I could, but then I'd just have to find somebody else."

"I think I could solve that too, Ariel. Before I became a producer, I had a management firm. Just a few clients. As a favor to you I could take your career in hand and gradually build you into a major star."

"Marty's going to be disappointed."

"Think about yourself. Look to the future. You sign with me and let me make the big decisions."

"I want to think about it," she said.

"This lightning won't strike twice," he said. "Take it or leave it."

"I'll take it," she said, "but I want a new contract on *King's Harbor*."

"You're my client. Consider it done."

He held out his hand and she took it. When they rose, he gave her a fatherly peck on the cheek.

Pat was having his second cup of coffee while waiting for Lana. Her mother, with her habitual cigarette dangling from her lips, sat across from him engrossed in the Calendar Section of the Los Angeles Times.

Mabel looked up and asked, "These people been in touch with you?"

"What people?" Pat asked.

"Says here they're doing a movie of the week about Lyla Taylor. Looks like they'd put you and Lana on as consultants."

"We wouldn't be much help to them," Pat said drily. "We still haven't gotten to first base on this one."

"You haven't come to the right place," Mabel observed.

"Don't let her get started," Lana said as she entered the

room. "Mom can rehash the plots of every mystery from Edgar Allan Poe to Sue Grafton."

"So who killed Lyla Taylor, Mabel?"

"I thought you told me Bette Davis did it," she said.

"We've checked out every Bette Davis look-alike in town."

"What about those female impersonators? Some of them you couldn't tell the difference."

"We've been to every transvestite bar in town. No luck."

"So you two are going to sit here in my kitchen and drink my coffee for the rest of the day?"

"No," Lana said. "We're going to check out those places that sell masks on Hollywood Boulevard."

Pat parked the car in the lot behind Musso & Frank. He and Lana dined there frequently, and the car jockeys knew them and didn't bother to charge them.

"We'll be back for lunch," Pat said.

"*Si, amigo,*" the ticket taker said with a smile.

Coming out onto Hollywood Boulevard, they skirted around a drunk lying on the sidewalk. A shifty-eyed young man leaned against a parking meter and looked away quickly rather than make eye contact. He obviously knew they were detectives. A nice-looking young couple, clearly honeymooners, loped along the street peering into windows and trying to find Hollywood and Vine where they would have their pictures taken under the street signs.

Harry's Novelty Shop was empty of customers when Lana and Pat entered. As far as the eye could see were Mickey Mouse figures, whoopee cushions, tee shirts with vulgar messages, replicas of Grauman's Chinese Theater, funny postcards, publicity glossies of dead movie stars, and other junk of interest only to tourists. The entire back wall was covered with masks of celebrities old and new.

The man who emerged from the back room wore an umbrella hat and a gardenia in his lapel which squirted water if someone came within striking distance.

"What can I do you for?" he asked. "I've got a special today on wind-up dildos."

"I've got more of those than I can use," Lana responded.

"How about you?" the proprietor said to Pat.

"I'm more interested in masks," Pat said.

"You've come to the right place," the proprietor said.

"Let's see what you've got in the Bette Davis line."

"I haven't carried Davis in I can't remember when. Is this for a party or something?"

"Not really," Lana said.

"Most calls I get these days are for Madonna or Ricky Martin. Want to take a look at either one of them?"

"We're only interested in Davis," Pat said.

"I'll see if I can order a Davis for you," said the proprietor.

"Actually we're detectives," said Lana. "Have you ordered a Davis mask for anybody else recently?"

"Nope," he answered. "What's this all about?"

"Murder," Pat answered.

Curtis Hughes could hardly believe his luck. He could walk right onto the Magnum Studio lot by showing his ID tag now that he was a member of the kitchen staff.

His parents had bugged him about finding another job after he'd been fired from his parking valet job. He told them he had filled out applications all over town. In truth, he had applied only at Magnum Studios. It was the only place he wanted to be. Close to her.

Most of his duties consisted of carting dirty dishes from where they had been collected by the waiters to the washing machines. But once in a while he was ordered to help clear tables after diners had finished their meal. At such a time he searched the room carefully to see if she might be there, but so far he hadn't seen her.

He learned that she took her lunch in her trailer when he noticed a tray with her name on the ticket. She had been there only a short time, but already there was competition to see who would deliver her lunch tray. Sam, the guy who had been there longest, usually got to deliver trays to various dressing rooms. It was a choice assignment because it meant you could get out of the steaming kitchen into the fresh air for a while. Sam always came back from delivering to Ariel's trailer with a big tip and a vivid description of how much breast he had managed to glimpse.

Curtis had to bargain with Sam before he finally had his chance to make the delivery. He had to take Sam's place at the garbage disposal detail twice and pay him five dollars to boot.

He arrived at the trailer trembling with excitement. When he heard her voice telling him to enter, he almost dropped the tray.

She was sitting on the built-in bed at the rear of the trailer studying her script. She had on some kind of slinky robe that opened slightly as she turned.

"Put it anywhere," she said.

Rather than place the tray on the side table, he walked toward her with it and tried to place it on the small footstool in front of the bed. It enabled him to look down into those twin mounds of delight which had been described in such detail by Sam when he had come back from this assignment.

"Not here," she said with a smile. "Over there on that table. Here, let me move some of that stuff away."

When she rose, a mist of warm, aromatic perfume moved with her. He breathed in and almost fainted. The plates on the tray rattled as he set it down.

She was looking at him.

"You're new, aren't you?"

"Yes, I just started."

"Have I seen you somewhere before?"

"I don't think so," he said.

"You look like someone I know."

"I look like a lot people."

She dismissed him then by signing the ticket and adding a tip. As he went out the door she noticed he had a slight limp. For the life of her she could not remember where she had seen him before, and then she went back to studying her script.

Emory Goode had just come back from giving Robin's dog Oscar his nighttime walk. He gave the dog his customary biscuit. Oscar yawned and laid down on his cedar-lined bed.

"Good night," Emory said, and closed the door to the kitchen.

He was making his way toward the desk, intent on going over tomorrow's filming and hoping to tire himself enough that he might sleep, when a timid knock sounded at the door. The white Lab seemed to sense a friend; rather than barking belligerently, he stood at the door and wagged his tail expectantly.

He hoped for a moment that it might be Robin. He was not disappointed, although a little surprised, to see Roberta.

"I was just in the neighborhood," she said with a tiny smile.

"I'm glad," he said. "Come on in."

"Just for a minute. I know you have to be up early to get to the set."

"No matter," he said.

"Would it be just awful if I asked you for a drink?"

He poured her a glass of cognac from the bar and one for himself.

"Cheers," he said, and then both sipped the liquor.

"I spent the last four hours just walking along Hollywood Boulevard."

"No sign of her?"

"No, and I just keep wondering if she's even alive. None of the young people I talked to claimed they'd seen her."

"We could run over and try some of the shelters again," said Emory.

"I tried every place I knew about." And then, in an attempt to brighten the conversation, she said, "Tell me what's going on with you." But before he could speak he saw that tears were slowly brimming over, and he reached out and took her in his arms.

"We mustn't give up," he said.

"We can't," she agreed.

"I've got your shirt all teared up," she said and started to withdraw from his comforting arms. He drew her back to him and after a long time, as if by mutual agreement, the comfort turned into wanting and they moved into the bedroom.

CHAPTER TWENTY-THREE

"I s Mr. Porter expecting you?" Elena asked the little
man who had rung the bell.

"No, but tell him it's urgent, Elena."

"You're Mr. Miller, aren't you?"

"Yes, we met at the *King's Harbor* party."

Elena returned a moment later and led the agent through the
house, out onto the deck, and to the side of the house where a
spacious hot tub was concealed in a grove of tropical palms and
plumeria bushes. The aroma of night-blooming jasmine mingled
with the scent of the sea.

"What's so urgent?" growled a voice rising from the steam.

"Why don't you just cut my heart out?" Marty said, his voice
trembling with emotion.

"Come on, Marty, we're not on television here. No need to
put on an act. What's eating you?"

"You're killing me, Max. You take away the first good client
I've had in years and leave me nothing. I can't let you do this!"

"Marty, you cut a rotten deal for that girl. You ought to be
ashamed of yourself. She deserves better."

"Then give her a better deal, only let me deliver it."

"You're not even a good messenger boy, Marty."

"What have you got against me, Max? You've done nothing
but humiliate me every time we've been together."

"You really want to know?"

"I really want to know."

"First of all, you're an agent. That's already strike one. And you're not a good agent. That's strike two. And you're an ass kisser, and that's strike three and out."

"Max, I'm begging. Give me a break."

"Get on your knees, schmuck."

Marty slowly knelt and looked imploringly into the hot tub. Max was floating now. His immense hairy belly visible, pink and steaming from the heat. For the first time some sign of pleasure crossed his face and he smiled benignly.

"Get out of the business, Marty. You don't belong in it. It's only for people with guts."

"Please, Max."

"Go home. You disgust me." In a loud voice he called, "Elena!"

She arrived almost at once.

"Show Mr. Miller to the door, would you, please?"

Elena led the way. The man seemed almost blind, and when she looked at him more closely, she saw tears streaming down his cheeks.

"I hate talk shows," said Justin Hargreaves. "I don't watch them, and I don't go on them!"

"Justin, I need a favor here," said Addison Snow, the head of the publicity firm retained by Porter Productions. "Max is driving me crazy."

"He drives us all crazy," responded Justin.

"It's the 'Gloria Blackstone Show.' You know she's on coast to coast now. Ratings almost as good as Rosie's."

"I've got nothing to say," Justin said.

"But you say it so well," Addison said. He knew Justin would come around with a little persuasion. He was no different from any other writer. They were all secretive and paranoid and filled with all sorts of resentments. Justin, even though he was moderately successful, was no different from the rest.

"You'd really save my life, pal," Addison said. "Max's threatening to pull the account unless I get him one major interview a week."

"What's the subject Miss Blackstone is trying to destroy this week?"

"She's doing a show about television, but I hardly think she wants to destroy it. After all, she eats off it. Anyway, she's a pussycat. She wouldn't destroy anything. If it's money you're looking for, there's an honorarium of five hundred bucks."

"If I needed five hundred bucks, I'd rob a bank."

"So you'll do it, Justin?" Addison asked.

"I'll let you know," Justin said. "I've got another call waiting." And he hung up the phone.

The other caller was Max Porter. He was calling from the lobby of the International Broadcasting Company.

"I saved your show," Max said in his wheedling voice. Justin knew the tone of voice. Max was going to try to sell him a bill of goods.

"Just had a meeting on *King's Harbor*," Max said.

"Why wasn't I there?" Justin asked, making no attempt to hide his resentment.

"I've got to level with you, Justin," Max answered. "Your old friend Sherwin feels you have not been responsive to his notes lately."

"His notes wouldn't even make good toilet paper," Justin said.

"There you go," Max said. "You shouldn't have said that to him, but never mind. I listened and here's what we have to do. Are you taking this down?"

"I'm listening."

"In the scene with Ariel the first time we see her, Sherwin wants her dressed in a flesh-colored leotard so it looks like she's naked."

"I already told him I wouldn't do it," Justin said.

"You just changed your mind," Max said. "He also wants a little more steam in that bedroom scene between Ariel and the lifeguard. He wants it staged so it looks as if it was filmed through a potted palm. That way it'll look like they're doing it."

"Absolutely not," Justin said. "I didn't create these characters to act that way, and they're not written that way."

"Then rewrite them. I'll expect those pages on my desk by the time I get back to the office."

Justin was sputtering furiously, but it did him no good, for Max had already returned the phone to its hook. In a flash Justin knew what he had to do if he were going to face himself when he shaved in the morning.

"Addison, it's Justin," he said when the other party answered. "Put me on that talk show."

Justin was still smarting the following morning at six a.m. as he was being made up to appear on the "Gloria Blackstone Show." Gloria Blackstone was a young black woman, one of the new breed of talk show hostesses known for her incisive questions and genuine interest in truly exploring the subject at hand. He had not yet met her, but the make-up man was filling him in.

"Gloria? She's an angel!"

"Then how come everybody's so afraid of her?"

"Who said so?"

"It's what I've heard," Justin said.

"Don't believe a word of it," the make-up man said as he jabbed a sponge full of flesh-colored pancake make-up under Justin's eye.

"This will lighten your eyes. They're all sunk back in your head."

"I've been working nights," Justin said.

Just then a disarmingly innocent looking woman appeared at Justin's elbow.

"I didn't expect a writer to be so handsome," she said. Justin was immediately charmed. Even under the make-up he could feel his face flush.

"You're Gloria?" he asked.

"Special guests I escort right to the stage. We're going to make an entrance," she announced.

"Okay by me," Justin said, feeling suddenly very good about himself.

With her arm in his, they entered the studio where an audience was responding to a stagehand who held up a sign that read: "Applause."

After about nine minutes of commercials, the program announcer said, "And now, here she is, the Queen of Talk Television, Ms. Gloria Blackstone."

Wild applause and cheering from the audience. Gloria rose and bowed graciously. By the time the applause had died down she was seated in the hostess' chair beside Justin Hargreaves, who was enjoying the attention.

"Our guest today is one of the most important people in our industry," said Gloria. "He writes pilots. You have seen his work, and you will be seeing a lot of it this fall when *King's Harbor*, his newest series, goes on the air. He's one of those people who works behind the camera, but his contribution is just as important as those of the actors we see in front of the camera. Everything we see and hear on television is scripted. In the beginning is the word, but how little we cherish those who provide the word! Today we are going to remedy that, and Justin Hargreaves is going to take us behind the scenes and into his heart. Justin, first, what is your personal view of television?"

"I came into television writing with the greatest of hope and expectations. I thought it could change the world, and I wanted to dedicate my life to it. I felt proud to be part of it.

"Television could have been used to inform, to educate, and to humanize us all. Instead, it has become a cesspool."

Gloria had not hoped for such a controversial answer so quickly, but recognizing it, she welcomed it and decided to go with the flow.

"You sound as if you have a good many negative feelings about our industry. Ours is a violent society. Certainly you don't hold television responsible?"

"I certainly do, for a lot of it."

"But you are television. You are The Writer. You are one of those who puts the words into the actor's mouths."

"Only words the people at the networks and the adverting agencies want there. If it doesn't sell a laxative or a sanitary napkin, the words have no use and they are cut or changed or the show is canceled. Lately, it's gotten even worse."

"Then why don't you get out of it and do something else?"

"I've gotten very used to eating in good restaurants, and I keep hoping that, in spite of it all, something I write might somehow fall on fertile ground and make a small difference in somebody's life."

There was a flurry backstage and an assistant came to the edge of the stage with a cellular phone. He pointed to Justin, indicating that he was wanted on the phone.

"We're on the air," objected Gloria imperiously.

The assistant again indicated that it was an urgent call.

"It's the head of the network. He insists on speaking to your guest," said the assistant.

"Go to commercial," said Gloria in a resigned voice.

The screen filled with a picture of a pitch man who called everyone Vern and invited the audience to join him at some automotive center in the county.

Gloria was looking at Justin with ill-concealed dismay, and she listened shamelessly.

"I don't give a damn what you say, Sherwin," Justin was saying. "I'm not retracting anything I said."

"You'd better settle that before we go back on the air," observed Gloria.

"Fuck you, Sherwin," said the writer and hung up the phone.

"I don't think we're going to continue this interview," said Gloria.

"I have no intention of continuing this interview either," said Justin. He rose, jerked the microphone away from where it had been attached to his shirt and strode out of the studio.

Max was waiting at the office when Justin arrived. Justin had never seen him this angry. He was so angry, he was calm.

"You're out of here, schmuck," said Max.

Justin looked past him into his office. It was empty.

"Where are my things?"

"They're out on the street, and that's where I want you."

It was almost with relief that Justin walked down the stairs, out onto the street, and sat down in his office chair on the sidewalk. He would call a moving truck eventually, but for the moment he simply enjoyed a huge sense of freedom and relief.

In the evening, the street turned into a neon nightmare, and the blare of the canned music caused the little kiosk to throb with sound and motion.

Robin had been busy making smoothies and single juice orders, but now in a lull between orders, the need for the cocaine began taking over her body once again.

She tried drinking orange juice to slake the thirst that overwhelmed her, but it didn't help. When the tingling and cramping became almost unbearable, she decided she had to take some action.

"Could you advance me twenty bucks?" she said to the

swarthy man at the front of the counter.

Alfredo, the Mexican owner of the juice stand, looked at her with compassion.

"Sure, I could advance you a little, but I'm not going to do it. You'll just run to that dealer over on Curson Street and get a fix."

"All right, it's true," said Robin. "But I'll die if I don't get it."

"Let me do this, little girl," said Alfredo. "You got a family in this town?"

"They don't understand," she said.

"They'll understand you need your mama and poppa right now. I'll get someone to take over here, and I'll take you home. Just tell me where you live."

Robin gazed at the man woefully. He didn't understand either. He was like all the rest of them who had never been hooked. She unwrapped the apron and the little beaked hat Alfredo had supplied her. She laid them on the counter and moved away. Alfredo looked after her sadly. Another lost child on Hollywood Boulevard.

When she reached the corner, she was seized with a trembling which she couldn't control. She put her arm around the street light in an attempt to steady her body. When the seizure had subsided, she began walking again, holding out her hand and asking for change from the other strollers on the street.

One of them placed a quarter in her hand, but others swore contemptuously or simply looked away as they rushed on past.

The man in the expensive convertible was her father's age. He cruised slowly along the curb, keeping pace with Robin until she came to a red light.

"Can I give you a lift somewhere?"

For a moment she considered. He might have a bag, but he didn't seem like any of the other coke heads or dealers she knew.

Seeing her hesitation, he was encouraged, and in a less nervous voice, said, "Anywhere you want to go."

"I don't know," she said.

"Would twenty dollars help you out?"

She had been on the street long enough to know what the twenty dollars would cost her.

He leaned over and opened the car door invitingly, and she nearly got in in order to satisfy the terrible need that possessed her. When she looked at the man, she saw his lustful longing, and even though the money would ease her pain, she could not face the degradation. She shook her head and went on down the street, pleading with strangers to give her a dime or a quarter.

Max was still in the hot tub when Emory Goode arrived. He had stayed in the water longer than he had planned. His strategy had been to persuade Emory to get in tub with him and to put Emory in a more receptive mood for the budget cuts Max wanted to make.

By the time Elena announced him, Max was ready to cool off, but he lingered hoping that Emory would join him.

"I don't think so," said Emory when Max suggested his guest join him. "I'm in enough hot water already."

"Oh come on, Emory. It'll relax you."

"Exactly what I don't need if this is a business meeting."

"Emory, Emory, Emory, would I hold a business meeting in a hot tub?"

"If you wanted to disarm a director who has gone over budget, you bet you would."

"Now that you mention it, Emory, you have already gone $50,000 over. You didn't need to build that new skating rink for that one scene. I could have had Justin rewrite the script and put the scene in an existing set."

"I needed that skating scene. I needed to show Ariel and Derek in a beautiful setting and show their growing attachment to each other. Besides, you've used the existing sets so much the audience is bored with them."

"I'm just telling you, Emory, you go over another cent and I'm getting myself a new director."

"I've got a contract, Max. I'm not letting you out of it. You knew I was expensive when you hired me. Money is quality, and you and the network said you wanted a quality piece of work."

"Not if it's going to cost me the national debt. If you've got any fancy plans, you'd better tell me about them now."

"Listen, we're on the verge of a major hit. We've got Ariel, people are going to love her, you'll get your money back the first season. You won't even have to wait for syndication. Advertisers will be begging to get on the show."

"From your mouth to God's ear, but one more cent over budget and it comes out of your pocket."

"Don't ruin this show with your usual cheap tricks, Max," Emory said. He turned and made his way across the deck and back into the house.

Max reached up on the pool deck and picked up the phone. The anger had left his voice now. His tone was brisk and businesslike.

"Sam, I'm taking your client off my show. He's already gone $50,000 over and he won't give any assurance that it won't happen again. If you've got any suggestions for another director, let me know."

He was returning the phone to its receiver when a hand holding the phone cord slipped it quietly over his head. It began slowly to tighten around his neck.

He thrashed in the water for a minute or two and finally he was still. The last thing he saw was the face of Montgomery Clift.

Justin was still in a rage when he arrived back at his apartment. He felt cheated and victimized. How dare Sherwin or Max tell him what to do with his characters! They belonged to him. He had created them. He was the Creator. The Creator giveth and the Creator taketh away. When he came to that realization, Justin knew exactly what he had to do. He had to take away the role of Tiffany by any means possible. He was pissed with Ariel, anyway. She had barely given him the time of day since they had cast Tim Dean as Derek. He should have known better than to trust an actress. They were fickle and had no sense of loyalty.

He also realized that he would have to do the rewrites Sherwin and Max had asked him for in order to regain his job and access to the lot.

He poured himself a drink and began to write.

Elena recognized Justin Hargreaves the minute she answered the door. She remembered his bringing her home from the party and the wild lovemaking that had taken place in the limo and the consummation afterwards in Max's bed.

They looked at each other shyly for a moment. And then they both smiled.

"I've been hoping you'd come by."

"That was a lovely nightcap we shared."

"He told me you'd quit."

"There was a misunderstanding," he said. "Is he around?" he asked.

"He's in the tub."

"Why don't you give him this script? Tell him I've fixed it the way he wants it and the way the network wants it. Tell him I flew off the handle, and I apologize."

"Wait here. He may want to see you."

She had been gone for only about a minute when Justin heard a long, horrified shriek. He followed the sound of the woman's voice to the deck, and then across it to the Hawaiian grove.

Elena was pointing into the hot tub where Max's body floated.

"He's dead," she said.

Justin gazed calmly down at the body.

"He finally got what he deserved," he said.

★　★　★

It was first light when Pat O'Collins and Lana Slocum drove across the bridge from the Colony and out onto Pacific Coast Highway.

"Money can't buy happiness," Pat said with a yawn.

"It can buy you a pretty imposing house, though," Lana observed.

"Wonder where people eat breakfast in this neighborhood?"

"Wolfgang doesn't open till lunchtime."

Pat guided the unmarked car into the lot of Denny's and they joined the early morning crowd of surfers and truck drivers.

Lana ordered fresh fruit and black coffee. Pat had the Number Three Special, scrambled with bacon, cheese, sausages and hash browns.

"So do you think the butler did it?" Lana asked.

"No," answered Pat through a mouth full of scrambled eggs. "I've always been looking for a murder where that would be the case."

"The maid might have."

"If it was her, who could have left that side gate open, and why?"

"She could have left it open on purpose just to throw us off."

"I don't think she's on our list. There's no motive. He was her bread and butter. And she impressed me as honestly in grief for him."

"Could be remorse."

"Maybe, or a good acting job. At any rate, we'll get a better idea about her once we see what she stood to get in his will."

"I'm more suspicious of the agent," Lana said.

"Well, he's a possible."

"So's the writer."

"But it was Emory Goode who last saw him alive."

"It's getting to be a habit. I think we'd better pay a call on Mr. Goode before anybody else."

"Just let me finish these hash browns," Pat said. "They're really crispy. Just the way I like them."

On the back lot of Magnum Studios, a strange-looking creature was moving through the area called "the jungle." She was thin and dirty and most of her face was hidden by an extra-sized straw hat. She was known as the "Cat Lady," and all anyone really knew of her was that she was given entry to the studio to feed the hundreds of feral cats that lived on the back lot. The cats were allowed to make their home there because they kept down the rat population.

Emory Goode was watching the Cat Lady while he had his first cup of coffee of the morning. Today he had resolved that he would do his best to keep within Max's budget, even though in his mind he was compromising the project just a bit.

He was not expecting his agent this morning and was surprised to see Sam Wells appearing through the mist, walking around the man-made lake Emory was using for this scene. He had substituted a swimming scene in place of the ice skating scene he had originally planned to use. The studio had provided him with a lake free of charge.

Sam Wells was one of the new breed of agents, educated, bright, observant, dedicated to serving his client but also to understanding the problems and needs of the producers who were the buyers. Sam and Emory had respect for each other and were friends.

They shook hands warmly, and Sam also drew himself a coffee from the machine.

"Let's move off a little. We have to talk," said Sam.

"You're here early. Is there a problem?"

"I had a phone call last night from Max Porter. He told me you've been a pain in the neck and too free with his money and he's firing you."

"I'm not surprised. He was really gross and threatening last night when I was over at his house."

"He means it. You and I have to decide what we want to happen. I don't think it's a good thing for you to be fired."

"Neither do I."

"I think you're going to have to pull in the reins and try to come in under budget."

"I've already tried to accommodate Max. I know he's tight, but he's also got a company to run and he's got to show a profit."

"I think we can get Max to change his mind. Go on filming today and I'll get to him as soon as he'll see me."

Coming around the lake, Emory spotted two familiar figures.

"What are they doing here?" Emory said, indicating the two detectives.

"I don't know," Sam said. "Who are they?"

"They're the cops investigating Lyla Taylor's murder," Emory said.

"You folks must like show biz to be up and around so early," Emory said.

"We'd like to ask you a few questions," Pat said.

"If it's about Lyla Taylor, I've told you everything I know," Emory said.

"Where were you last night between seven and eight o'clock?"

"I was in Malibu," Emory said. "I had a business meeting with Max Porter."

"What business did you discuss?"

"We discussed today's filming. What's this about?"

"Did you and Max disagree about anything?"

"Max and I always disagree."

"What is this all about, detectives?" Sam asked.

"Max Porter was murdered last night."

Ariel Smart disrobed with a sense of pleasure in her body, remembering the lovemaking of the night before with Tim Dean. He had been gentle until they both went beyond thought and reason and into a zone of pure feeling. Afterward he had held her until they both became drowsy and fell asleep.

He had still been asleep when she awoke, but she woke him with a kiss. He immediately wanted sex, but there wasn't time, as much as she would have liked it. He promised to stop by her trailer before reporting for his own make-up call later in the day.

Ariel allowed herself to bask in the warm memory of the lovemaking and dropped the silk robe to the floor. She enjoyed the sense of total freedom that her nakedness gave her.

She reflected on all the things she had to be thankful for at that moment. She had won a starring role in a network nighttime pilot. She was in love with a man who returned that love. She had allied herself with a powerful producer/manager, and there was hardly another girl her age in Hollywood with such a bright future. She was proud of herself that she had attained this level in her career and now seemed about to ascend to real stardom.

She was looking at her image in the mirror critically and objectively. The figure was trim, the legs were long and well formed, her breasts were upright and firm. She touched them briefly remembering the pleasure Tim's touch had given her there.

Ariel could not account for the sudden feeling of discomfort. Had she detected some quick, unexplainable movement in the room? Did she imagine it? A physical feeling of apprehension began at the nape of her neck and extended down her spine.

She shivered, although it was not cold in the room. She could not explain what made her quickly reach for her robe and throw it over her shoulders.

On the pathway approaching Ariel's dressing room Emory Goode, too, was discomfited. Why was that figure lurking behind the actress's dressing room? At first he guessed the man might be a greensman trimming the oleander hedge that grew behind the little wooden house, but as he drew closer he saw that the man, more a young boy, had his eye pressed against the side of the building and was peering inside.

The boy was so intent that he didn't hear or see Emory until Emory had him by the collar and was hauling him around to the front of the building.

"Let me go, mister. I was just looking for something."

"You're a peeping Tom. What were you looking at in there?"

"Nothing."

"Then let's go take a look together."

The boy tried to squirm away, but Emory held him even tighter and forced him over to the door.

"Ariel, are you in there?" he called.

After a moment, the surprised actress opened the door and called, "Good morning," but then she saw that Emory was restraining a young man.

"What's going on?" she asked in confusion.

"Your dressing room isn't as private as you think it is," Emory said.

Unconsciously Ariel wrapped her dressing gown around her more tightly and at the same time looked more closely at the young man.

"Where have I seen you before?"

"I bring your lunch every day!"

"No, I realize now I've seen you lots of times."

"Well, I work on the lot," he said.

It then dawned on Ariel where she had seen the kid times before.

"He's the guy who's been stalking me and my roommate," she exclaimed.

Her recognition seemed to open the need for confession. "I don't give a hoot about your roommate. You're the one I care about. I've followed your career all along. You wouldn't be where you are today if it weren't for me. I've done things for you. Some day you'll find out about them."

"I think we'd better call the studio cops, Ariel." Emory said.

"Please don't do that," pleaded the young man.

"Sorry, son, you can't do this kind of thing."

Ariel went back into the dressing room.

"Come on, mister. What's wrong with wanting to see a pretty girl naked?"

"What's wrong is—-it's without her knowledge and without her permission."

"Didn't you ever love anybody?"

"I'll answer that if you tell me what you meant when you said you've been doing things for her. What kind of things?"

The boy seemed about to go into the fetal position, but he was pretending. He punched Emory in the solar plexus so hard that Emory nearly doubled over. But he held on to the boy even harder and said, "Try that again and I'll break your arm."

"My dad's a lawyer. When he finds out about this he's going to sue you and everybody here."

"I hope he's a good lawyer. You're going to need one."

"You're going to be sorry for this, Mr. Goode," the boy said.

When the cops came Curtis fell silent and would not respond to any further questions. He allowed himself to be led away as if he had lost all will to resist.

Robin Goode had walked all the way from Hollywood Boulevard to reach the house in Laurel Canyon. She had been there often before when Lyla was alive.

Now, as she passed the workers from the Water Department, she paid no attention to them, nor they to her. They continued working over the open manhole where a generator was pushing fresh air down into the opening.

She knocked on the door to the house. When there was no response, she walked around to the side entrance into the back yard. In her need she seemed alternately hot and cold. One moment she was shivering, the next she was removing her sweater.

The hillside behind the house was thickly planted with tall eucalyptus trees underplanted with a mass of chaparral. The eucalyptus aroma was irritating to the sensitive membranes of her nostrils, and she removed a handkerchief from her pocket and covered her nose with it.

She was grateful to spot David Taylor immediately. He was swinging in a hammock stretched between two trees. She thought he was asleep, but in truth he was watching her behind lidded eyes. Just as she came abreast of him, he jumped up and said, "Get the hell out of here!"

"It's me, don't you remember?"

"I remember you never show up unless you've come to beg."

"This time I've got money," she said.

"Two dollars, four dollars, don't bother me, little girl."

She reached in her purse and removed a small roll of dollar bills.

"I don't even want to know how you got it."

"I'm working now," she lied. "That juice bar on Hollywood Boulevard."

"Oh, sure," he said and turned away toward the house.

"Please," she said. "You've got to help me."

"How much have you got on you?"

"Ten dollars and some change."

"Let's see it."

Robin handed over the roll of bills and was reaching into her pocket for the coins.

"Keep the change," he said. He rapidly flipped through the bills. "Wait here," he said and entered the house.

Alone now she took a tissue from her purse and began blowing her nose. The prospect of a fix seemed to calm her, and she paced slowly back and forth on the patio. The aroma of eucalyptus was overpowering and had almost a drugging effect of its own. She breathed in deeply and wished for the seconds to pass quickly.

David Taylor returned in his own time, cruelly aware of her need and what each second's deprivation cost her.

He held the small plastic sack of white powder over her head in a macabre teasing game.

She made one futile grab for the cocaine before he relented and placed it in her hand.

At that moment there was a sharp whistle in the underbrush up on the hillside above the flagstone patio. In the same instant the workers Robin had passed on the way in swarmed over the fence and into the back yard. One of them yelled, "Police! You're under arrest."

Taylor attempted to run into the house but was stopped and handcuffed before he reached the door. Robin tried to throw the packet into the plantings at the border, but it was too late.

When she saw the policeman approaching her with the handcuffs dangling she began running in a circle. Once he restrained her, she screamed incoherently. She was still screaming and resisting when they placed her in back of the police car and took her away.

Roberta was working on a landscape job on Rexford Drive in Beverly Hills when the call came over her cellular phone. She did not even both to explain to her assistant, but ran to her car and drove recklessly to the hospital in Century City.

Emory was waiting, his face strained with concern and grief. He explained that Robin had collapsed at the Hollywood Station and that she was under treatment in the detox center. That was all he could tell her.

CHAPTER TWENTY-FOUR

The house could have existed in a Rockwell painting. On Valley Spring Lane in the San Fernando Valley, it was a two storied tall structure with white shutters looking down across a fresh green lawn. Maple trees dotted the lawn and flower beds were just bursting out with spring flower bulbs. The only thing wrong with the picture was that two plainclothes detectives were standing at the front door. One of them was ringing the door bell.

The woman who answered the door was dressed in a blue pin stripe suit. Her hair was short in a stylish efficient cut and her face showed the care and attention of at least one plastic surgery.

"We're Detectives from Homicide," said the stout male detective. "I'm Pat O'Collins. My partner is Detective Slocum."

"What can I do for you?"

"We're looking for Curtis Hughes."

"What do you want with him?"

"Just want to ask him some routine questions."

"Routine questions about what?"

"We think he might be able to shed some light on a case we're working on," Pat said.

"I'm his mother. He's in the back yard. Come this way."

Mrs. Hughes led the detectives through an attractive, well-furnished, formal house to a patio where a man was fanning coals in a charcoal grill. In a hammock was a young man looking vacantly up to the sky. His hands were clasped behind his head.

He came quickly but guardedly to attention when his mother ushered the two strangers out into the yard.

"These people want to ask you some questions," his mother said.

"Hold on there," said the man at the grill. "What kind of questions? Who are you, anyway? What's he done?"

The detectives introduced themselves and explained that they would like to question Curtis alone.

"I demand to be present," said the father. The boy for the first time showed some reaction. He became sullen and indignant.

"It's all a lie," he said. "Whatever they're going to tell you. It's all a lie."

"We had a report that your son has some information about the murder on the Magnum Studio lot. We'd like to find out what that information is."

"You know anything about this?" Daniel Hughes asked his son.

"There's this actress I like over there. She's a friend of mine. I was visiting her, and the studio cops grabbed me."

"Why don't you just tell us what you know about the murder."

"I saw it! I was there!"

For the first time, his mother showed some reaction. She looked to the boy in surprise and disbelief.

"Tell us exactly what you saw," Lana said.

Curtis' father said, "You don't have to tell them anything."

"I don't mind," Curtis said. "I've been wanting to get it off my chest."

Lana Slocum took out her notebook and began taking down information as the boy talked.

"I was parking cars at the Ivy. These people came out. I heard them say they were going out to the studio. As soon as I could get away, I followed them."

"Who are we talking about?"

"That director, Emory Goode, and the woman who was try-ing out for the job on *King's Harbor*, the girl that got murdered."

"Why did you follow them? Why were you interested?"

"I wasn't going to murder her. I was just going to fix her so she couldn't get the job."

"What did you have against her?"

"Nothing special. I just wanted the job to go to somebody else."

"What had you planned to do to her?"

"Rough her up a little. Maybe give her a black eye, just some-thing to keep her from getting the job that was meant for Ariel Smart."

"I don't believe any of this," said the boy's mother with a sig-nificant look at her husband.

"Yeah," said the father, "I don't think we're answering any more questions."

"I want to," said the boy.

"Go ahead," said the stout cop. "Those studio gates are guarded. How did you get on the lot?"

"I started a fire. All hell broke loose. Anybody could have got-ten on the lot that night."

"What happened after you got on the lot?"

"I'd been there before, and I knew where the set was. Emory Goode and Lyla Taylor had already been there for a little bit, long enough for him to start coming on to her. She's really a slut, but I'll say in her favor she didn't want Emory Goode to make out with her. He forced her back into the bedroom set. She was fighting him every step of the way."

"Did she cry out? Did she resist?"

"Oh, sure, she cried bloody murder, but those stages are soundproof and nobody could hear her. Finally," Curtis said, "he got her down on the bed, but she wrestled herself away and started running. When she ran through the kitchen set he grabbed a knife and tripped her and then went to work on her with the knife. I got scared then and beat it."

"Why didn't you come to us and tell us what you saw?"

"I was scared. I'm still scared."

His mother and father looked from one to the other in dismay.

"You should have seen this coming," his father said. "If you'd paid any attention to him all these years, he could have been like other boys!"

"Me?" his mother said indignantly. "You're the one who neglected him."

"You're the one who insisted he go to that damn camp."

The boy looked at the cops as if he owed them an explanation.

"It's where I got the polio," he said.

Oblivious to the cops and the boy, mother and father continued to hurl insults at each other.

"If you'd remembered to take him for the damn shots, he'd be normal today," said the father.

"Why didn't you do it, you bastard, you're his father!"

"We'll need you to come with us to the station to make a signed statement," Lana said to Curtis.

"Ready when you are," Curtis said.

"You folks can come with us if you'd like," she said to the parents who barely heard her above the sound of their argument.

"Let's get the hell out of here," said Curtis.

They were halfway out the yard when the mother called, "We're coming with you."

"You're a little late," he said.

Emory had come straight to the apartment from the hospital. The dog greeted him eagerly, and he was putting the leash around its throat while he listened to his phone messages. There was only one.

"Emory, this is Elena Gomez. I wonder if you'd stop by to see me as soon as you can. Thanks so much."

The minute the message was over, the phone rang. He picked it up.

"It's Ariel," she said. "Are you okay?"

"I just got home. I'm fine."

"Emory, something happened and I think you ought to know. I don't believe a word of it, and I don't think you're involved in any way."

"You've got my curiosity up, Ariel."

"The police just left here. They were looking for you. They think you killed Lyla. Someone told them they saw you do it, and they're on their way to your apartment to arrest you right now. They think you killed Max, too."

"Where are you, Ariel?"

"I'm at the sound stage. Marty's coming by, and Justin's back in his office and says he's got something to tell me as soon as he finishes work."

Emory was startled by the ringing of the doorbell.

"Thanks, Ariel," he said and hung up the phone. He tried not to panic. He wondered who his accuser might be, but he also knew that if he were arrested, he might lose time which would better be spent in clearing his name. He rushed to the back door and checked to see if anyone was there. The way was clear, and he hurried down the stairs.

While he had only been questioned by the detectives about Max Porter's murder, he had never felt he was completely clear of suspicion. He had tried to reason who else might have wanted Max dead. It seemed to him that there might even be some connection with the murder of Lyla Taylor.

A different Elena answered the door to Max Porter's house. She had dropped the posture of a subservient domestic worker. Instead of a maid's apron she now wore a bathing suit covered by a long bathing house dress. She might have stepped off the cover of *Vogue.*

Emory tried to conceal that he hadn't recognized her immediately.

"Elena?" he asked.

"Come in, Emory."

He entered and followed her to a small sitting room overlooking the ocean.

"How have you been?" Emory asked.

"In mourning," she replied with a wry smile.

"Max and I were not close," he said, hoping to gain her confidence.

"We were too close," she answered. "Let us be honest. He was a mean bastard, and I don't know of anyone who is really sorry that he is gone."

"Have you any idea who killed him?" Emory asked. "It's suddenly become terribly important that I find that out."

"I suspected you at one point," she said.

"I didn't do it," he answered.

"I believe you," she said. "I think if you were going to kill a man, you'd do it face-to-face and not hide behind a mask."

"I'd like to think that too. What makes you think Max's killer wore a mask?" asked Emory.

"I'm not sure he wore it, but I did come across one hidden in the flower bed before the cops got here. Would you like to see it?"

"I would," answered Emory.

She led him to a small shed adjacent to the Jacuzzi. From a shelf she removed something covered in a plastic bag. From the bag she removed a torn water logged mask of Montgomery Clift.

"Have you told the police about this?

"I don't need them around here anymore," she said.

"Where did this come from? It didn't belong to Max, did it?"

"No."

"Unless I miss my guess, this is from a collection of masks of famous people. I saw it in an exhibit in Santa Monica many years ago. You can see how well made it is. People who collect Hollywood memorabilia go crazy for this stuff. Its not all that expensive, but the mask-maker is dead now and his pieces are rare."

"But why would he be wearing a mask in the first place?"

"Obviously so nobody would recognize him."

Emory tried to remember more about who had owned the collection of masks. It seemed to him that when he saw it the collection had been for sale. And then he had a second idea.

"Gerald, this is Emory Goode," he said into his cell phone.

"You're doing good work, Emory," Gerald said. "I like this pilot a lot. Thanks for coming back on the project."

"Sorry for cutting straight to the chase, Gerald," said Emory, "but I need to pick your antique collector's brain."

"Go," said Gerald, pleased that he did not have to make a stupid decision about some silly-assed television show.

"You know the Yamashura Mask collection, I'm sure."

"Beautiful things. Lovely things. I would have bought the collection intact, but somebody beat me to it a long time ago."

"And who was that?" asked Emory.

And when the executive told him, Emory floored the accelerator. He had to get somewhere quickly. Somebody's life could depend on it.

★ ★ ★

Night was falling fast as it does in California. In her dressing room, Ariel Smart was waiting impatiently. Justin had called and said he was making some last-minute changes in the scene she was to film tomorrow.

Ariel was uneasy. Nothing had been normal since Max Porter's murder. Emory Goode had been off somewhere on some personal business, and now the police had insinuated that he might even be the killer. She didn't think he was guilty, but at the same time she was uneasy. She wondered what would become of the pilot if things didn't get back to normal soon.

Now she was alone. Night was falling and she wished she were home. It was that time at the studio when all the day workers have gone home and only a skeleton crew carries on the nighttime operations. When footsteps sounded on the stairway up to her dressing room she turned to see Marty Miller. She could tell even before he spoke that he was distraught.

"We've got to talk," he said.

"If this is about you wanting me to sign with you again, I think it's a lost cause."

"No way, baby," he said. His voice was becoming low and threatening. She had never seen him this way before. Usually he was pathetic and pleading.

"We've got a contract, Ariel. You try breaking it, and I'll tie you up in court so long you won't be able to play Grandma Moses."

"In case you don't remember, Marty," she objected, "I never signed that contract. It's unfair, and you might as well know I'm not going to have anything more to do with you."

"I've done more for you than you'll ever know."

"Then I thank you for that, but don't do me any more favors."

"Then let me appeal to your better nature." Marty was back in his pathetic mode. "Let me tell you the truth. I've overspent, Ariel. I owe alimony, office rent, house rent, child support, you name it, but I had faith in you and I spent a lot of time on you, for both of our sakes. I spent time on your career. Time I could have spent on other people. I've sacrificed for you. I've done things for you that you will never know. You owe me."

"Max said you made a terrible contract for me. He said you sold me down the river."

The agent's face flushed. "If I hadn't represented you and pushed you for that role, you'd be a waitress at Denny's."

"But I've never had to wait tables. I was doing just fine in New York, Marty. I don't want to go on with this conversation."

"I thought you had a heart," he said. "I guess I was wrong."

He turned, and at the door she could see that his face had turned ice cold. For a moment she felt pity, but then the expression in his eyes disturbed her, and she knew she had been right to sever all connection with him.

After he left, she felt a sense of great uneasiness and foreboding. She decided not to wait any longer. She picked up the phone and called Justin.

"I'm getting tired of waiting. Are you going to be much longer? If so, I'd like to go home."

"I've only got one more page to write. It won't take me long." He said.

"I'll wait," she said, but she grew tired of waiting and decided to walk to the production office. She wondered what he wanted to see her about, anyway.

Darkness had fallen now, and the mist of a California evening gave a moist, murky thickness to the air.

She had gone only half way to the production office when she saw a figure coming toward her in the darkness. It was a man, and he blocked her way back.

"Who's there?" she called.

The figure did not answer but continued toward her. When it was a few feet away she recognized the face of the actor, Anthony Perkins. She tried to go in the direction of a street light, but that way was blocked by the man. With a frightened sob she plunged into the darkness behind her.

She had come to that part of the lot referred to as the jungle when she became conscious of the chorus of tree frogs. She had to be wary because the artificial lake was somewhere ahead of her. But she realized it too late and slipped from the embankment into water that came up to her waist.

She remained there trying to still her gasps for air. And when she became quiet and held her breath, she saw the silhouette of her pursuer moving along the pathway only a few feet away.

Perkins moved cautiously and stealthily, seemingly unaware

of how close he was to her. After hesitating briefly, he continued on toward the street where old western movies had been shot. It was a ghostly old set of clapboard false fronts with weather-beaten buggies and wagons sitting in the darkness.

After a time, Ariel lost sight of him and began to breathe again. She moved as quietly as possible out of the water and back up to the path. She was tempted to call out for help, but she knew that a call would be overheard by her pursuer.

Once out of the water, she waited until there were no footsteps, no sign of the man, and she felt safe enough to try to find her way back toward the light.

When she came to the Midwestern Street she felt safer, but in the bandstand that stood in the center of the town square she thought she saw him again.

She ducked into the doorway of one of the old Victorian house exteriors. Something rubbed against her ankle, terrifying her. When she reached down, she startled a cat which leapt off the porch with a shrill cry.

At the same time the figure on the bandstand rose and started towards where she cringed in the doorway. When he came closer, she saw Anthony Perkins clearly.

This time she tried to run toward the guard gate where she knew she would find help. The masked figure was almost at her heels when she fell sprawling into the grass.

When she looked up she saw two figures grappling with each other. She rose to her feet and, almost paralyzed with fear, watched while one of them struck the other, knocking him to the pavement. The figure remained there unconscious, and a knife went clattering down the pavement.

Emory held out his arms and she ran to him sobbing. "It's all right, Ariel, he's not going to hurt you now."

"Who is he?" she cried.

He knelt down and pulled the Anthony Perkins mask away from the unconscious figure and there revealed in the light of the street lamp was the face of Marty Miller.

Hurried footsteps sounded in the darkness. Emory turned to see Pat O'Collins and Lana Slocum approaching.

"Mr. Goode, we have to ask you some questions regarding the death of Lyla Taylor."

"I think you might want to talk with this gentleman first," Emory said, pointing to the prostrate figure at his feet.

No one was more astonished than Emory Goode when he received a message from Marty Miller who was in jail awaiting trial. "I need to see you," said the note, and on the appointed day Emory found himself sitting across from the prisoner.

"Thanks for coming," Marty said.

"I can't imagine what you want from me," Emory said.

"I need a favor," Marty said, "and somehow I think you'll understand."

"What do you want?" Emory asked. In spite of what the man had done, Emory felt some small degree of pity for him.

"I need you to understand something," Marty said. "Maybe then you'll do what I ask."

"I'm listening," Emory said.

"I used to be a good agent. I used to joke and say I'd kill for my clients," Marty said. "And then everything went bad. Client's left me. My wife soaked me for all the alimony she could get. I couldn't even pay the rent and ended up living in some crummy little office cooking on a hot plate. And then killing for a client wasn't a joke anymore. I finally had to do it. I figured if I got rid of Lyla Taylor, Ariel would get the job on your pilot and she did."

"Pretty drastic solution to your problem," Emory said. "What did you have against Max Porter?"

"Have you ever been humiliated?" Marty asked.

"In this town, in this business, every day!" Emory said.

"Max stole the only client I had working and then he spit on me. I hated the son of a bitch!"

"And Ariel," Emory said. "Did you hate her?"

"I wasn't going to kill Ariel," Marty said. "I was just going to fix it so she'd never work in this town again. After all I went through for her, if I didn't get those commissions, nobody else was going to get them!"

"So what do you want from me?" Emory asked.

"Under the doormat outside my office is a key that will let you in. In the back of the closet there's a little wooden chest. I want you to burn everything that's in it."

"What is in it?"

"Me."

"You'll have to tell me more than that."

"It's my dark side, the side that let me do anything I wanted to as long as I was reenacting a scene from a movie. It wasn't really me that killed Lyla. It was a character in a movie. It was Bette Davis the way she did it in *Hush, Hush, Sweet Charlotte*. And it wasn't me that killed Max Porter. Did you ever see what Monty Clift did to Shelley Winters in *A Place in the Sun*?

"He drowned her."

"Just like that mask let me drown Max!"

"And what did Anthony Perkins have in mind for Ariel Smart?"

"The same thing he did to Janet Leigh in "Psycho". That chest is full of masks that would let loose demons if I was to ever wear one of them again. Burn them for me, Emory."

"I'll destroy them, Marty," Emory said after a long thoughtful moment. "Once I'm sure they're no use as evidence I'll set a match to the whole collection."

"Don't worry," Marty said with a grim smile, "I'm not going anywhere."

It was three months later when Robin Goode came to the

gate of the Hillsdale Substance Abuse Center. She found two familiar faces waiting. Purple Hair stood to one side of the entryway, and her mother was walking up the street towards her.

"I'm surprised to see you," she said to Purple Hair.

"I've called every day to check up on you," he said. "They told me you were getting out today."

Roberta stopped a few feet away, not sure whether or not to interrupt the conversation.

"I've got a new place," Purple Hair said. "It's out at the beach. Nobody but us."

Roberta heard the boy's offer and she waited. She felt like murdering the kid, but at the same time she wanted Robin to make her own decision. She felt as if somehow her daughter's life depended on what she decided now.

"I'm going home," Robin said looking to her mother, and then back to the boy. "Thanks for coming today, but you ought to go home, too."

The boy smiled, "I don't know where home is anymore." He gave her a rueful smile, then turned and walked away.

Robin rushed to her mother and they embraced.

"You look like a new person," Roberta said.

"Nope," Robin said. "Same old person, but patched up and clean and on my way back. I was hoping Dad would be here, but I guess that was asking too much."

"He knows you're getting out today. I spoke to him earlier."

"Nothing changes, does it," Robin said ruefully. She picked up her bag and started toward her mother's car. They both spotted the Bentley approaching at the same time. Emory pulled up beside them and said, "I'm looking for my girls."

"You nearly missed us," Roberta said.

"Why aren't you working?" Robin asked.

"I finished that job. If you two are in the mood, I've got tickets on a cruise ship that leaves from Auckland, New Zealand, for Fiji and points beyond.

"I've always wanted to see 'points beyond'," Roberta said.

"I've always wanted to see Fiji," said Robin.

"Then both of you get in the car," said Emory. "We've got a plane to catch."